"Shocks, Meester?"

stories

Robert Perchan

SPUYTEN DUYVIL

New York City

Library of Congress Cataloging-in-Publication Data

Names: Perchan, Robert, 1947- author.
Title: "Shocks, meester?" : stories / Robert Perchan.
Description: New York City : Spuyten Duyvil, 2023.
Identifiers: LCCN 2023026830 | ISBN 9781959556664 (paperback)
Subjects: LCGFT: Short stories.
Classification: LCC PS3566.E68 S56 2023 | DDC 813/.54--dc23/eng/20230622
LC record available at https://lccn.loc.gov/2023026830

PART TWO:
MEMOIR INTROMISSION

PART THREE:
OTHERWHERES

PART ONE:
THEM OLE TIME
SPLIT PENINSULA BLUES

THE ARTIST STORY
ROSE IN THE STEEL DUST

"*I am lonely, Oggie.*"

"You can come with me to Brad's for my Saturday afternoon beer and talk to Ronni."

"I don't like bar talking scene. Always can make me be boring."

"Bored, sweetheart."

"Everybody this town think I dumb. Even Ronni. And she Number One *dumb*."

"Well, who do you want to talk to? That goddam madam from Youngstown? Jesus!"

"She nice Korean lady."

"She runs a massage parlor, for God's sake."

"Is health spa."

"Right. Suzy Wong's Health Spa: Oriental Massage. Visa and Mastercard accepted."

"Suzy *Kim*. She rich lady. Got Benz. Big Hand is customer at there."

"It's *boji* bumping and *jaji* jumping, Jang-mee. And everything in between."

"Shut the mouth! Don't talk that kind way. We do for each other. And we just poor."

"You're talking crazy now. Are you on the rag already?"

"All of time you say such shits to me. 'Rag already.' I am lonely, Oggie."

"You've got lots of friends."

"You friends. Nice guys but all of time talk about art. Want friend can know life feelings."

"Baby, life is Art."

"I don't care!"

Jang-mee continues making a quart of grape juice, spilling a dollop of the dark purple concentrate on the zipper-flap of her jeans. A fine spring morning, but I, August Finch, have been up all night welding the steel-tubing flower stems to the floor of the birdcage. The Summer Show is in early July this year and I am behind schedule. Jang-mee crosses the kitchen to the sink in a deliberate plod. Not a morning goes by that I don't take stock of my life. It all makes sense until that moment I ran across a book in the library by an American woman missionary titled *I Married a Korean*. Jang-mee crushes the cylinder of frozen syrup in the bottom of the glass pitcher with a wooden spoon. Adds water. I was looking for a book on Korean celadon pottery, the exquisite if monotonously greenish-bluish stoneware. I had seen only a couple of pieces close up at an exhibition but had been impressed by the single-mindedness of purpose that had gone into fashioning and firing them. Imagine doing the same thing generation after generation for untold centuries. Jang-mee stirs the gloop into a uniform mixture–grape juice. It would take a year, I was told, before I would see any signs of progress. Gradually she would come around. Begin to appreciate the delicious privacy of American life that had seemed like an imprisoning isolation. Jang-mee taste-tests, sipping from the hollow of the wooden spoon. She wept nightly for the first six months. Homesick. Homesick for a family that despised her for marrying a foreigner. Homesick for a family that despised her for taking a job in a "cocktail corner" where she might come into contact with foreigners. For doing anything but sit at home like a lump of dough waiting to be punched into the shape of a dutiful housewife to a Samsung Service Center drone. Jang-mee pours two glasses of grape juice. She is waiting for me to tell her what I want for breakfast. I have been up all night. I want to drink blood and acid. I want to pick my teeth with roach limbs. I want to explain. I drink the grape juice.

"I am lonely, Oggie."

I am lonely too, darling. And it's not your fault.

Sit down here with me here for a while, stranger, and listen. If I had the money I'd buy you a round. So let's "go dutch." Did you know that "going dutch" is an extraordinarily humiliating experience for a Korean? Only *one* of the parties must pay for the whole group. Any other way makes everyone feel cheap and miserly. Three Koreans leaving a bar will stage a mock struggle at the cashier's counter until one of them puts on a good enough show of plenty to pick up the tab. Potlatch, I think it's called. Something like that. But they always know whose turn it is to pay, deep down. And, to give them their due, they always know who has fallen on hard times and needs a break. That "deep down," however, is unfathomable to us outsiders. A foreigner is not expected to be able to comprehend it. Hence he drinks a lot of free beer. Am I boring you? Well, this is Brad's. Don't expect to run into the Ancient Mariner in here. That's C. over there–The Towering Wino one wag dubbed him one night, though he doesn't drink any more than the next guy. He's a grump, these days. Lonely, but he won't admit it, being a man. Don't bother talking to him unless you're a Charles Bukowski fan and can remember back when poetry actually meant something to people. And that's Ronni down at the end of the bar. She models for the advanced drawing classes sometimes. I think she tried to pick me up one afternoon, the first time Jang-mee took off for Suzy Kim's, but I was too thick in other thoughts to catch on. I mention it here only to show you how I just let things happen. Or not happen. The only reason I got to go to Korea was the original guy took sick. Hepatitis. Here in the States. Right here in Southeastern Ohio. Athens, for God's sakes. (Phidias T. Bluster I nicknamed a loudmouth ex-stonemason classmate of mine.) So they looked around at the other graduate students in Sculpture and saw me sitting cross-legged in a corner fashioning my lawn ornaments. Just the right guy, they must have thought. Not engaged in anything serious. And they were right. In half an hour I was in the library thumbing through *I Married a Korean*. Korea! I thought. A niche! And every artist needs a *niche*. Spend a year in a place nobody ever thought of going. Come back with an exotic tale or two. Virgin princesses with tiny silver suicide daggers hidden in the folds of their lustrous gowns. Shamans who descend to the Underworld and return with bodings dire or tidings auspicious. "Celibate" Buddhist monks driving around in SUVs and talking on handphones to horny housewives. That kind of weirdo thing you hear about when you mention to people you're headed East. But I didn't drag you over here to tell you that. It's Jang-mee I'm worried about. She's lonely, like she said. But you can't understand this loneliness. I barely can. And if I said *They're not like us* you'd want to label me a you-know-what. And maybe you'd be right, these days. And I really can't see that I've done anything wrong.

Of course anyone can see where all this is headed. I return home after a few words with "Number One dumb" Ronni, perched on her barstool with her legs crossed. A Flapper body if there ever was one. They have them in Korea in spades. Flat chested. Low slung narrow hips. Clunky ankles and knees though. Yet deliciously gracile in their own way. Nymphic. Jang-mee, naturally, is gone. Pulled up stakes again. I could tell you about *her* body too. The first time I saw her naked I was dumbstruck. I had been working on her for weeks, coming to her "cocktail corner" and suffering fools buying me free beers just to get a chance to talk to her privately, in confidence. She worked in a joint in Seoul called the United Nations Club, a spacious cushy hall harboring a dozen small horseshoe bars, each manned (that word doesn't sound right) by a young woman who smiles and chats at whatever trio or quartet of Korean salarymen shows up to be chatted at. I showed up too, a couple of times a week, neglecting to order the $10 plate of dried squid snack that was–I learned later–her bread-and-butter menu item, the one she got the most commission on. It took a while. Korean women are not likely to model nude. Seems Confucius was against anything that put one's dead ancestors on edge off in their Never Never Land of piss and gloom. So I told her about my idea for my Our Lady of Ashes. Reclining, as on a deck chair. Naked, naturally. Skin surface the scorched texture and gray-black of campfire ashes. I was serious and she must have appreciated that. So we did it, the modeling sessions I mean, but no further than the nervous preliminary sketches. Incredible, nevertheless, her torso, that taut and faintly tumescent rectus abdominis. Then she stopped coming to the little studio apartment I had rented. Disappeared. Like now. Had to think things over. Battle it out with her family. Lose. Despair. Take up, ultimately, with the foreigner after all. It happens that way a lot. Ask her. I can give you her new address.

A fine spring day, like I said. Up all night welding the steel-tubing flower stems to the floor of the birdcage. Upstairs Jang-mee has torn all her clothes out of the chest of drawers while I sulked at Brad's, my socks hanging out like drooping tongues. She's been careful enough to leave the business card of Suzy Kim's Health Spa: Oriental Massage on top of the chest. Address and phone number. Rescue me, perhaps. Perhaps not. On the carpet, the six stainless steel Norelco rotary razor blades I was intending to affix to the tips of the steel stems like gun-metal corollas. Crushed. Stomped flat. Like flowers pressed in an iron book. Jang-mee, by the way, means "rose" in Korean.

The circular blades had raised radiating cutting surfaces that met the floating heads of the electric shaver just so. Little multi-armed steel swastikas. When I first arrived in Seoul I wanted to find a bookstore. I needed a book, any book. Met a student on the street who spoke no English but wanted to be helpful. Koreans can be like that. He drew a map of downtown indicating the locations of the big bookstores by drawing tiny encircled swastikas. Told him if I wanted to buy a copy of *Mein Kampf* I'd have stayed in America. He didn't understand. Later I learned a swastika—fiddled with in your brain a little–is also a Buddhist symbol of "well-being." Very old. Going all the way back to the Sanskrit *su-asti*, "be well," something like that. And all the way up to the modern day Thai *sawas-ti-ka* greeting. It's all there in the guidebooks if you care to look it up. You see them everywhere painted on temples, Buddhist bookstores, and there was a big pink neon one outside my studio window. Of course they don't really mean shit, being a symbol. A week after the swastika episode I read in an English-language newspaper that the leader of one Korean Buddhist order knifed the leader of a rival order. To death. The Ven. MacHeath. I would have to order more blades. I sit down at the typewriter and do a little white-lie begging for Art:

Not so long ago I requested that you send me six (6) Norel-co Type 0-7611 Rotary Razor Blades. I remitted twenty-five dollars ($25) by money order to cover the cost and postage and handling, but as of this writing I have yet to receive said merchandise. I realize that you are a large concern and that my request is somewhat out of the ordinary. However, if you will allow me, I will explain my intentions and give you sufficient reason to comply with my order ASAP.

I am a sculptor, as yet unknown but with every intention of having my work represented in all the better contemporary art galleries in the country and overseas in a matter of a few short years. The sculpture I am currently engaged upon is one that will both honor Nature and yet do justice to those advances and improvements upon Nature made by such progressive and reliable firms as yours. The project, which I call "The Rose in the Steel Dust," could be briefly described thus: A large old-fashioned steel birdcage. Emerging out of the center of the cage floor will be twelve (or thirteen) stainless steels tubes varying in size from 1/16th in. to 3/8th in. in diameter. These are "stems" of the flowers. On the ends of six (or seven) of these tubes will be affixed steel alligator clips of varying sizes. One of these clips will be placed so that it is "biting" into and breaking–or seeming to break–one of the metal bars of the cage. On the remaining six (or seven) tubes *will be affixed six (or should you be so generous, seven) of your patented stainless steel Rotary Razor Blades, suggesting an abstract form of a complex hermaphroditic flower. Should you be so kind as to fill my order as soon as possible, I will be well on my way to creating a work of Art that will honor both Nature and Technology and perhaps open the eyes of those who have chosen to detract from one in order to pay excessive lip-homage to the other.*

Gratefully,
August Finch, Sculptor

Outside I dump the rolled up bedroom carpet on the apron of the driveway. Empty half a can of Charco-Lite on it. Wait like a good suburban husband for the juice to soak in. That's all she ever wanted, maybe. A good suburban husband. Bringer home of the Bacon Bits. New car every three years. Colleges for the kids. Drop a lit match on the pile–POOM! Now that, my friend, is FIRE. On this very carpet we first made love in America. Different from making love back in Korea, where it was like penetrating a seamless matrix of womanhood. A web. "Screw one, you've screwed them all"–there's something to that, but not in the way it's usually meant. The apron is ablaze now, a thick, black layer of smoke oozing out the rubber pad on the underside of the carpet, wafting toward Mrs. Musgrave's next door. The black smoke is not just smoke— it's also fingernail-size flakes of licorice soot, sticky-looking. Old Mrs. Musgrave appears at her picture window, cane in hand, three-legged, as the black flakes begin to dapple her quaint white house. Jang-mee seemed smaller here in the States, the first time we made love on the carpet. As if she'd lost mass and volume, shrunk, on the big hop across the Pacific. I didn't think much about it at first. Just that she'd need a little time to grow, gather strength from the humanoid dynamo that is America. Like they do with astronauts when they come back with spongy bones from a two-week jaunt through the Big Empty. Old Mrs. Musgrave continues staring, staring. Probably thinks I'm charneling Jang-mee's corpse out here, wrapped up in the carpet like tamale filling. And she wouldn't be too far wrong. In the ashes a form begins to emerge, a torso and a pair of stumpy limbs. When would Jang-mee begin servicing her first customer up at Suzy Kim's—tonight? Tomorrow afternoon? The very month we hit the States an article appeared in a men's magazine detailing the operations of a vast nationwide network of massage parlors, whores, mama-sans, and pimps, all Koreans. The FBI tried to eavesdrop on their interstate phone calls—nab them for conspiracy in the name of the Mann Act—but they couldn't crack the carefully coded Korean slang. I let Jang-mee see the article, moving her lips as she untangled the English. She pronounced it horseshit. Such a thing could not be. Right on cue a police cruiser appears at the top of the street, creeps slowly down North Congress toward me and the house I rent and therefore don't pay taxes on. The officer behind the wheel rolls down his window. A good sign. It's when they lumber out of their shells like mutant turtles that you know you're in for a hassle. "We've had a complaint." "Sir?" "By city ordinance citizens are not allowed to burn trash in residential areas." Citizens? I am rising in the world. "We don't intend to cite you. But this *is* a warning." And your brethren up in Youngstown don't intend to cite Suzy Kim and her nationwide network of pimps and madams either, do they? But I don't say that. "I didn't think the trashmen would pick it up. Too big." "There's a dump out on Route 8." Brother, don't I know that—I've got a couple of aborted pieces out there on display right now. But I don't say that either.

Jang-mee has been going up to Suzy Kim's more and more often of late, staying a little longer each time. Of course I didn't mean that crack about her servicing her first customer. She says she just talks there, with the old lady and the girls. There is no Suzy Kim in actuality.

It's just a World of Suzy Wong name, like I kidded Jang-mee. And it's curious that it's usually artists and whores and other entertainers who have separate professional names–here and in Asia as well. Even I had one, in Korea: *Mu-hak*. Which can mean either Dancing Crane or Ignoramus, depending on which Sino-Korean characters you choose to represent the sounds. And it fit–what with my long, spindly legs and my ignorance of the culture I was bathing myself in. The madam's name at Suzy Kim's is Mrs. Hong. The girls who work for her all married and divorced GI husbands. Married them in Korea, divorced them over here. On the grounds of unreconcilable cultural differences. Or is it "irreconcilable"? *Mu-hak*, like I say. And I'm no writer. It's just that everyone has one story in him, or her, at the least. And I'd like to shave as close as possible to things as they are. Divorced. Sex as a glue loses its adhesiveness 30,000 or 40,000 feet up over the Pacific. Thank God 747s aren't riveted together with Sex. Or maybe some of them are. One of the girls comes down and visits Jang-mee occasionally. They first met in church, of all places. I've heard that's where immigrant Korean women head when they start to lose their bearings and marbles. And where massage parlor madams hang out, angling for pecker fodder. She's not so bad, really, the girl. A little firecracker. She and Jang-mee talk, and they talk, hours on end. All night long. Marathonian. I grilled Jang-mee afterward one time, after Jin-hee (or Ginny, as she's Americanized it) had left.

"Why'd she get divorced?"

"She lonely."

"Oh? She's happy now?"

"Is better."

"It's better working in a massage parlor?"

"Money better. Friends better. Food better."

"Food?"

"Can eat Korean food all of time."

"Food is *that* important?"

"You don't understand. All of things can be imported." She meant *important*.

"And love? Is love important?"

"Love is all of things. Not separated thing."

"I see."

"And GI husband beat her up. She too much cry make his Momma angry. So beat her up."

Well, I thought back then, at least there was one atrocity I hadn't committed. Though Jang-mee once told me she finds it difficult to respect a man who doesn't raise a hand against his wife once in a while, when she is wrong. Go figure.

In the living room on the tube David Frost is interviewing a withered crone who looks a lot like Mrs. Musgrave. Or vice-versa. A rerun, either way. She is talking about Paris and the Lost Generation days. Hemingway. F. Scott Fitzgerald. That madman Ezra Pound. I guess Henry Miller came later, bless his wandering soul. Did she know Gaudier, I wonder? Not Likely. Dead long before his time. All Frost and company can talk about is the "specialness" of Hemingway's feet. What did he have? Hooves? Flippers? Paws? Suction cups? Where's Jangmee? Has she really picked up and left for good this time? Every time she takes off for that place, she stuffs her overnight bag a little bit fuller. Of course I know I'm losing her. There's not much you can do when your rival is an entire culture. A way of life said to be five thousand years old. When your rival is the woman's own soul. I never should have made that crack about her going on the rag. It's just that I had been up for 26 bleeding hours straight. Or that crap about Life and Art. And I know I'm not considerate enough, giving enough. But it's when someone is miserable, or in pain, that you want to be attentive, or diverting, or just pretend that nothing's seriously wrong. And yet you know. And yet you know you're not going to be able to talk about it. Put your finger on it. Or ever honestly hope to find the words for it. Because you know there's nothing really to be done.

THE GOTHIC STORY
WITH INTENT TO MARRY

For the third straight day the Englishman sat on a sofa in the lobby of the downtown branch of the Korea Nationalal Bank of Exchange. The bank employees who had watched him pick up Mee-jung after work for the past two months had glanced at him and smirked on that first day. Then yesterday they went about their business as usual, paying him no more mind than they would a potted plant. Today they plainly resented him. Couldn't he see that Miss Lee wanted nothing more to do with him? That she wouldn't show up for work until he gave up? At least that was their best guess. She hadn't called in sick, and when a senior colleague phoned her home, her mother burst into uncontrolled sobs. The girl had simply vanished. Mr. Choi in the Loan Section wondered aloud if one of the Bongo van teams hadn't snatched her off the street and sold her to a brothel. She would have brought one hell of price, he pointed out, with that body. But no one said anything to the foreigner. It was easier to blame him. Late in the morning on that third day, Mee-jung entered the bank, pale, unsteady, as if she had come face to face with a ghost. And she looked older. Infinitely older. The Englishman, who had expected his fiancée to rush into his arms, approached her warily.

"Darling, where in God's name have you been? I've been worried sick for three days."

"This morning," she said darkly, "I finally found the courage to do it."

"Do what?"

"Bite off a man's mool-gun."

The supervisor of Sangbok Shipbuilding: Payroll let Soo-hyun go to lunch a half hour early so that he could call on his older brother to discuss a matter of "family importance," but Soo-hyun spent the better part of his bonus time crossing and recrossing the sidewalk in front of the Korea National Bank of Exchange. She would be inside there now, sitting behind the Foreign Exchange counter, though he could not actually see her through the huge one-way tinted windows. More than anything, he hoped to catch a glimpse of her new fiance walking through the bank's electronic-eye doors to pick her up for lunch. This would be enough to stiffen his resolve to carry out his plan and win Mee-jung over. He had nothing against the foreigner personally, he told himself, and it went without saying a man of the foreigner's means could find another match with no trouble at all. Soo-hyun had taken a look at the foreigner's tax exempt status documents on file at the office and seen how much the shipbuilding company paid him as a consultant—and it was better than six times his own junior bookkeeper's salary. As if one man could be six times better than another man.

Of course, he knew very well why the Englishman had singled Mee-jung out from all the other eligible young ladies he no doubt chatted with every day at reception desks and information counters. Generally Korean women just turning twenty-two are at best "cute"—*kee-yoh-woh-yo*. Mee-jung was different. She was womanly. As womanly as a spoon is womanly and a fork is manly. He savored, for a moment, the originality of the parallel, but this then led him to wonder if he was manly as a fork is manly. He couldn't know for sure. Like most of his friends before they married, the first woman he had ever penetrated was a prostitute, the almost obligatory, ritual excursion nearly every young Korean draftee—even some of the other Christians—makes on his first night of leave. Nevertheless, he had consummated the transaction three times in less than an hour, prompting the girl—she wasn't but eighteen—to chuckle *Chagun gochoo ga mepda*. "The smaller the pepper, the hotter it is." Thank God, he had thought, that his poor dead mother could not see him now. In a shabby room in an even shabbier brothel on the outskirts of a dumpy little village. And strange that for him and most of his friends it was a whore who bridged that terrible abyss between mother and, ultimately, wife. And disgusting that some men returned and hung out on the bridge when they wearied of the closed-door intimacies of domestic relations.

The problem was that Soo-hyun, too, was out there on the bridge. And when he thought of this bridge, he was reminded of old Tarzan movies and their bridges of slats and twisted vines slung across precipitous chasms of certain extinction. Worse, it was getting more and more crowded out there on the bridge, and the price of just keeping your place—let alone getting all the way across to the other side—was going up. A bottle of beer at Cicada Heaven was up to 8000 *won* now, and the pricey platters of dried squid and sliced pear-apples which the girls served—and upon which they then feasted with ravenous alacrity—were growing noticeably less bountiful, as if all the squid in the deep seas and all the pear-apples hung in orchards had suffered from a sudden glandular disturbance, an epidemic of dwarfism. You could go broke out there on the bridge—and sometimes not even get to sleep with a *mae-mee*, a cicada, as they are called from their incessant chatter. Go broke, grow old—he was over thirty—and suddenly disappear, a pebble casually nudged off a plank into the downward blackness.

"I don't like it one bit, Soo-hyun. This is not the Korea of 200 years ago. Or even 20 years ago. We don't do things that way any more."

"But I must act now, *hyung-nim*. While she's still a virgin. Before it's too late."

"You know this for certain—that she's still a virgin?"

"I can feel it. In my bones." Soo-hyun was trembling, his flesh oily as a frying meat dumpling. "Before I lose her forever!"

"Little brother, I am a man of God. An ordained minister. A Christian."

"I'm a Christian too! And you are my brother. Help me."

"It seems to me that what you're proposing borders on rape."

"But rape *with intent to marry*. Your house would be perfect for the mourning period. The small room without the windows. Just for three days. Two nights. A kind of honeymoon. Until she's mine completely."

"Soo-hyun, it's tantamount to sin. I am a man of the cloth. This is a *rectory*."

"You are a Korean. If I don't act now she will marry the foreigner. And before they marry, he will seduce her. Try

her out like a pair of new shoes. You know those people—
their ways."

"It seems to me you are proposing much the same
thing."

"But I am a Korean. She is Korean. We are one blood.
One flesh. Can this be sinful? To want to possess her? It
is my birthright. You are my elder brother."

"I will think about it."

"*Hyung-nim*! I can't go on. I won't go on!"

"Not that again. Not those threats again!"

"I mean it this time. I really do!"

"Do you really understand what you are saying? Do
you have any idea what you are threatening? Your immortal soul!"

"*Hyung-nim!* I've applied for my annual leave starting
Monday. It's only three days. There's no time. Today's already Friday! We must act now!"

"I said I will think about it. Now go and wash your
face. It's as oily as your thoughts."

"Will you have lunch with me today?" Soo-hyun added, almost as an afterthought.

"I have an appointment."

"Please, *hyung-nim!*"

"I said I have an important appointment, Soo-hyun."

"I mean my *honeymoon*."

The Reverend Yong-hwan Gol leaned back in his heavy leather chair. Were it not undignified, even alone, he would have put his feet up on the desk. The rectory was a good place to think. He felt closer to God there than anywhere else. A younger brother was always a problem, a trial. They had few family responsibilities when young and this showed up later on in their character. Worse, they remained attached to their mothers—even dead mothers—to an almost indecent degree. Soo-hyun had wept uncontrollably for weeks after their own mother's funeral, and Yong-hwan knew he kept a photo of her in his wallet. A photo of her at a middle school class outing, of all things. The reverend often thought that the protection and aid that Confucian tradition required an elder brother to give a younger one merely contributed to the young man's spiritual delinquency. But Soo-hyun was no longer a young man. He was thirty-one and overdue to marry. The problem was that Soo-hyun's plan was an unChristian one—it was rape, plain and simple. The reverend pitied the girl, locked up for the three days and two nights in a small windowless room with a man in burial dress repeatedly violating her. Though, of course, any penetration after the first one was technically not a violation—for all spiritual intents and purposes she would already be his wife. And one could hardly "rape" one's own spouse—any more than one could pick one's own pocket, as the vulgar saying went. Still, it was not Righteous, and it certainly wouldn't be much of a honeymoon for her. But Christianity, he reflected, was a mere 2000 years old, a drop in the bucket compared to a culture that traced its roots to an origin twice as far back in time and then some. And the girl had been dating a foreigner for more than two months now, according to his little brother. That weighed in Soo-hyun's favor, in his plan's favor, morally speaking. Soo-hyun even reported that he had seen the girl take the foreigner's arm under their umbrella during a sudden cloudburst. She was, by Korean standards, little better than a foreigner's toy. Dead meat, spiritually speaking. Though Redeemable, of course. That was always Christianity's wild card. Still, again, the reverend did not like the plan. His wife and children had left for a weeklong visit to her parents, and he had hoped to use the children's absence to catch up on some reading and to finally call in the exterminators to knock out those pesky roach nests. He had been putting that off—the children were forever dropping their candies on the floor and then stuffing them back in their mouths. He didn't want his little son rolling a gooey gumdrop through a slick of roach poison. Kids will do the damnedest things. Now he would have to chuck those plans and set up the spare room for the mourning visit ceremony and "honeymoon." That in itself wasn't so difficult. And his only real responsibility would be to lock the door behind her when the girl entered the small room to pay her respects to the corpse. But there would probably be one heck of a racket for the three days and two nights until Soo-hyun broke the girl and made her a wife—for the first twenty-four hours anyway. And the handcuffs—*ugh!* Nevertheless, the reverend considered, marriage was forever, and once he got Soo-hyun married off he might finally get some peace of mind. And after all the girl was a fine woman, really, from what Soo-hyun said. She worked in a respectable bank. Her family name was a respectable one—unlike "Gol," which had been a burden for the reverend and his brother all their lives. (The Sino-Korean character representing the family name—骨—translated literally as "bone" or "skeleton," and they had had to endure no end of teasing and ridicule from their schoolmates in The Province.) He would be proud to have Miss Lee as a sister-in-law. It was just the stupid foreigner business—just bad luck that her flawless English had put her at the bank's Foreign Exchange Desk where she would inevitably collide with Western men. They were always creeping into the country and bringing about unpleasant situations like this. It was probably better to just get the whole thing over with soon enough. If he stalled, and the foreigner married the girl, he might never hear the end of it.

When Soo-hyun thought about the interview later, he realized he probably had a made a tactical mistake by threatening to take his own life. And he had neglected to tell his elder brother that his love for Mee-jung was genuine, even when Yong-hwan stressed that there were "other fish in the sea." He had planned to—love was to have been the very heart of his plea, the clincher. But it just didn't come out that way. Still it was hard to imagine that his brother wouldn't go along. The plan was simple, elegantly simple. And, he felt, touchingly beautiful in a way only an underappreciated office drudge lover like himself could understand. He even derived some satisfaction from the knowledge that Westerners—and probably a serious slice of his own countrymen to boot these days— might consider it cruel, even grotesque. *They* could never understand. Even Yong-hwan had become infected with some of their ideas. Christianity was fine—up to a point. He remembered the day a Mormon missionary told a group of English-conversation students that he thought the poem "Annabel Lee" was disgusting because the hero felt an erotic attraction to the corpse of his dead lover. Did

Elder Thomas—and "elder" was a mighty strange title for a 21-year-old college student—not know that filial piety required a Korean son to sleep in a special room next to the corpse of his father for the two nights of mourning before burial? *That this was an act of the deepest and most abiding devotion!* Soo-hyun had raised his voice to a foreigner on that occasion and was obliged by his fellows to bow out of the group, though he had been thinking of quitting anyway, ever since Elder Thomas gave him the nickname "Ichabod" and then chuckled to himself.

Soo-hyun turned into the small *boshintang* restaurant that he frequented with the other men from the office on occasional Saturday afternoons after work. One bowl was usually more than enough to energize him for Saturday night and Cicada Heaven. But he would need to start a few days ahead if he was going to keep Mee-jung on her back—and occasionally on her knees, "doggy" style, he imagined with a lip-smacking relish appropriate to his surroundings—for the three days and two nights straight in that little room without much fresh air except for the manacled trips to bathroom. That was the part Yong-hwan had most objected to, in fact. The handcuffs. Perhaps by the second night he would have broken her and he could let her do her female business unshackled. Wait and see. He would see it in her eyes. The submission. The love.

When the auntie set down the stainless steel bowl of steaming dog meat soup in front of him, there was something in her eyes that reminded him that eating dog, like drinking alcohol, without companions was the sign of a man in extreme desperation. So there was no other course but to barrel ahead and order a bottle of spiritous *soju*, as if he were a man who had gone utterly beyond shame and into a realm of purity that others could only surmise from a refracted distance. Also, he was thirsty. There were certain risks involved in the whole operation. She might refuse to come to his brother's house and light the obligatory joss stick beside his reclining "corpse." Yong-hwan was a minister and a persuasive man when he believed in what he was saying, and Mee-jung was a Christian, of sorts. But she could say yes she would come and then never show up. People were like that these days. No respect for the old ways. Or just lip-service at best. He would have to depend on his brother's powers of persuasion, his show of sincerity. And those powers were good. His congregation was devoted, as they say, a collection of lonely housewives and women desperate for meaning in a cold and calculating world with every reason to stay at home in bed on Sunday mornings, but they came to Yong-hwan's church and filled the pews.

Soo-hyun sucked on a particularly succulent slice of

dog meat—the auntie had been generous in ladling out his portion, perhaps because he was alone—drawing out the unique sweet juices that guarantee a man a night of stamina and penile durability under the bedcovers. Fattened in cages, the dogs were hung by their paws from a crossbeam and bludgeoned to death, a method which induced an internal bleeding that rendered the flesh particularly tender, especially about the loins. Foreigners, the English in particular, decried the practice, writing letters and campaigning, and Soo-hyun had heard the subject of *boshintang* was even brought up at diplomatic gatherings. He despised his own government for knuckling under and closing down the dog meat restaurants in the big cities for the duration of the Seoul Olympic Games last year, which was ridiculous because foreigners couldn't read Korean signs anyway. And what business was it of theirs what a Korean restaurant served? Fortunately the government compensated the populace by halving the yearly quota of Korean orphans released for adoption by foreign couples, buffing up its tarnished image as the world's leading exporter of unwanted babies. It was no secret that Americans and Europeans adopted Korean children to use as sweeps and houseboys until their innate love of freedom and hatred of tyranny matured and they rebelled, at which point the adoptive parents kicked them out onto the street, penniless and unschooled—sometimes even missing a kidney that had been transplanted to the couple's natural child. Such a victim, a woman, had returned from Sweden and told all on a television special, including the scandalous fact that she had been divorced three times by foreign men. They *use* us, he thought, dislodging with a matchstick a morsel of dog meat tucked behind a molar and then throwing down a glass of the sticky-sweet *soju* to cleanse his mouth of the debris. He had once read where a foreign man of letters had defined virginity as "just another form of ignorance." How long would it be before the foreigner dumped Mee-jung on the ashheap? Six months? Two Years? Ten? That would be worst of all—draining her of all her beauty and womanliness and then spitting her out like a spent husk.

He paid up and left, only now realizing—the *soju* was having its effect—what a fine, fine afternoon it was. There was little doubt Yong-hwan would cooperate. His wife and children were scheduled to make a trip to her hometown in The Province to see her parents. Filial piety. One more thing foreigners could never understand. It was not likely that his brother could decide that rooting out a few roach nests was more important than a younger brother's whole future happiness and welfare. Cockroaches, he thought. Before the outsiders had come with their pallets and warehouses full of Foreign Aid, Korea had been free of the pests.

He turned up the street and headed back to work. In the beginning he had dreaded going to the office in the mornings. He was from The Province—and people born in The Province were said to "arrive in the city with empty suitcases and leave with full ones." But things were changing. Things were looking up. More and more he was being invited to after-work drinking marathons, and whenever he judiciously—as a newcomer—introduced a topic into the conversation, it was taken up for serious, if drunken, consideration. This was a sure sign of social acceptance.

Still he had had to tread a little lightly in the office of late. It didn't look good that Supervisor Jang had rejected his recommendation that the Englishman Cruikshank be notified his marine engineering degree diploma was under verification review by "the authorities concerned." Soo-hyun had only wanted to inject a bit of Fear of Company Bureaucracy into the foreigner's soul. We lick their boots, Soo-hyun grumbled to himself as he stepped into the office. And then serve them up the virtue of our women. And only then did he notice that he had spilled three identical dollops of dog meat broth on his regulation blue neck-tie.

On Monday afternoon, his first official day of vacation, Soo-hyun sat on his brother's sofa in his loose hempen burial garments reading a magazine article about the imminent international trade war when his brother returned home from downtown. Yong-hwan was gazing at his wristwatch wearily, apprehensive yet resigned. He had worn his ecclesiastical collar to give his mission the proper air of solemnity.

"Soo-hyun cared about you deeply," the minister repeated for his brother the brief speech given Mee-jung a couple hours earlier. "Now he is no longer with us. But his dying request was that you should place a stick of incense in the censer beside his remains—and then forget him forever and go on to a new life of your own."

"What did *she* say?"

"She said she would come here directly after work. She said she was sorry to hear about your sudden illness. She said she saw you on the street last week and you looked fine."

"Is she coming?"

"I think she will. I saw her pick up the phone as I was leaving the bank—perhaps calling the foreigner to postpone an engagement."

"Their engagement," Soo-hyun said. "Forever."

"You had better get in your coffin."

And it was hard at this moment for the minister of the flock not to think of his little brother's threat of self-annihilation just days before. Perhaps, he thought grimly, too grimly he knew for a man of the cloth, I should have called his bluff. How many parishioners have made similar threats over broken hearts. And gone on to find contentment with the most unlikely of partners.

Soo-hyun had been practicing lying still in the makeshift coffin off and on all day. But this was difficult to do with such fiery anticipation in his loins. And the burial garments of coarse woven hemp didn't make it any easier. It was lucky for corpses that they're dead, he reflected. He had rented his costume for a tidy sum from a rather uncomprehending funeral broker. City people will do anything for money. And the corpse that wears these for real will have no idea what a "mourning" period he missed out on.

He settled into the coffin for what he hoped would be the final time that day. For comfort he had built it a little wider than what tradition called for, and he had positioned it a little closer than usual to the table on which he had set the censer. Suddenly he realized that the censer was empty and climbed out of the coffin again and lit a pair of joss sticks for effect. He didn't want Mee-jung to

think, even for a moment, that he hadn't had any mourn-
ers. He climbed back in and thought about how a woman's
body was like a coffin, carrying the seeds of dead gener-
ations into a new life. He dozed and had a fleeting dream
that Mee-jung was bestowing a kiss on his brow. His skin
tingled there, at the spot where the Buddha was said to
have a Third Eye. But that anticipation that was wired
deep in his nerves jolted him out of his sleep. Above all
things, he had to stay awake. He was gratified that the
tingle on his forehead remained. Perhaps his brief dream
had been one of those beneficent augurs, foretelling a loving and fruitful future. And then he heard the voices: the
curious sexual slur of Mee-jung's and his elder brother's
confident, consoling tones. No others. This was perfect.
She hadn't dragged along any of her co-workers from the
bank.

Out of propriety Mee-jung stared straight ahead and
did not glance at the remains when she entered the small
windowless room. She kneeled down before the low table on which had been placed Soo-hyun's framed photograph, a bowl of sacrificial apples, a vase of fresh joss
sticks, and the brass censer in which two sticks still smoldered, a sign that there had been previous visitors, though
the house had been queerly empty except for the elder
brother. She heard the door behind her close quietly and

the bolt shot to, but she did not think about it. Mourning customs varied. People from The Province can be a little strange. It would all be over in a few minutes and she would be back in Cruikshank's arms soon enough. She removed a stick from the jar and set it in the censer, lighting it with a match from a box set beside the table. She began her deep bow to the photograph, touching her forehead to the floor in reverence for the dead. Soo-hyun sat up slowly, stiffly—he'd been lying rigid in the coffin for nearly an hour. As Mee-jung lifted her face from the floor, she turned to look one last time on the corpse of the man who had tried to court her but whose affection she could not bring herself to return. The corpse was sitting up, breathing heavily and smiling at her, a fat brown cockroach with twitching feelers clinging to the center of his oily forehead like a scab before it lost its footing and skidded down his nose and dropped into the coffin. Mee-jung blacked out, pitching backward out of her kneel and landing flat on her spine, her legs falling slackly apart. Soo-hyun could see all the way up her skirt to the tops of her lifeless thighs. He was about to cross the bridge. A new kind of life was about to begin.

THE PICARESQUE STORY
KIMBOP'S STORY

Who is Kim—Kim—Kim?
Kipling

Lt. Varga: This the little fellow you wanted me to take a look at?

Sgt. Washington: Yes, ma'am. MP's picked him up over in Housing. He was riding around in circles on a bicycle belonging to one of Captain Capriati's kids.

Lt. Varga: How'd he get on base?

Sgt. Washington: Says he shimmied up the old tree over near the South Gate. Scrambled along a limb and dropped down on the Rec Center roof.

Lt. Varga: I can believe that. Look at the arms on him. What is he—some sort of pocket Tarzan?

Sgt. Washington: He's a mixed blood, ma'am.

Lt. Varga: Sure, but a mixture of *what*?

Sgt. Washington: Well, he's half Korean.

Lt. Varga: And?

Sgt. Washington: Your guess is as good as mine.

Lt. Varga: Has he got a name?

Sgt. Washington: He says it's Kimbop, ma'am.

Lt. Varga: Is that a Korean name?

Sgt. Washington: It's a kind of Korean food.

Lt. Varga: He's got to have a real name. You can't put "Kimbop" down on a report. He speak any English?

Sgt. Washington: He seems to understand well enough. But it's pretty broken. Or else he just isn't making any sense.

Lt. Varga: What does he say he was doing over in Housing riding around like a dervish on a stolen bike?

Sgt. Washington: He says he wants to get arrested. Says he thinks that will protect him from the Korean police.

Lt. Varga: Then turn him over to the Koreans. The little fool. The Code is posted in Korean on all four gates. This is not serious installation security business, Sergeant.

Sgt. Washington: I don't think he reads Korean, ma'am. He's some kind of orphan. They can't go to school if they—

Lt. Varga: Sergeant. This base isn't Boys Town. Contact the Korean authorities and take him to the Main Gate. If they want him, they can have him.

Sgt. Washington: He says they're not the only ones who want him. He says the Seven Eagles want him too.

Lt. Varga: Who?

Sgt. Washington: A local outfit. Pimps, mostly. Woman-selling. Protection. Blackmarketing.

Lt. Varga: Blackmarketing? Goods from the Commissary and Exchange?

Sgt. Washington: Yes, ma'am.

Lt. Varga: Does he know anything?

Sgt. Washington: I don't know what he knows, ma'am. I didn't have time to . .

Lt. Varga: Well, let's take a statement and turn him over. But I don't want the major to find out we wasted the morning interviewing some little underfed street monkey. On small potatoes. Neither do you. Understood?

Sgt. Washington: Yes, ma'am.

Lt. Varga: Kimbop, where's your home?

Kimbop: Can't got a home.

Lt. Varga: Well, where were you born?

Kimbop: Dongduchon. Mama got died at there Kimbop baby time. At later Gramma got died too.

Lt. Varga: Dongduchon?

Sgt. Washington: That's the village of Korean prostitutes up north near the DMZ. They service our troops up there.

Lt. Varga: Delightful. Kimbop, why don't you have a real name?

Kimbop: Got name only Kimbop, mam. The Yankee GIs calls me Kimbop because of I say name is Kim also I got a flavorite food is kimbop. You know what can be kimbop? Can be look like little log boil rice wrap in seaweeds with you can have chop pickle radish in a center or rich guy like Mr. Mo Tong Lark can be raw fish in a center he's. I know it. Did see it. Then can slice make little like wheels put in mouth easy and be lady gentleman. Some time a pushcart auntie can give Kimbop a kimbop come apart she no can sell. I just put in a mouth and bited it rice in a mouth sticky white like new teeth. That was ago. Now days I got a pocket money can go restaurant say Kim Bop Doo Geh, Joo Seh Yo. Mean kimbop two logs, please. And I don't got a pay at then. Pay after eated because of now days I got Mr. Mo Tong Lark Big Hand pocket money so restaurant uncle no think Kimbop cut and run. But not more longer. Now Mr. Mo gone a kill Kimbop. Or Police Chief catch. Same. So I here now come. Can be no place to Kimbop safety.

Lt. Varga: Who's this Mr. Mo Tong Lark?

Kimbop: Kun-son. Big Hand. Mr. Mo is of captain Bongo van team. Got four Bongo. Four team. Kimbop team can be of Smallpock Pang and Grabber Lee and Kimbop. Best team. Catch a most baek-boji of all team. Got a clamspse for a wrist hand of girl and clamspse for a ankles hold down. Girl no can go free of struggle. Just shake and moan scream. Grabber Lee grab she's panties scissor cut off stuff she's mouth so no scream more. Then she can see Smallpock Pang he's face she no scream because of too much scare.

Lt. Varga: Who's Smallpock Pang now, Kimbop?

Kimbop: Driver. Smallpock Pang we call he Smallpock Pang because of he's name can be Pang and he's school time he got a disease by smallpocks. So he work for Mr. Mo Tong Lark because of he can't got a job. He got too much holes in he's face and am ugly face man. May be he could of had was hamsome man but you got a wide holes in face everybody no want a see you on every day because of they gone a be sick at look of you. So you can get job catch a girl because of we catch a baek-boji some time she see Smallpock Pang he's face she gone a make a little shakes of she's whole body. She want a cry up but she's voice no can got out she's thoart and be loud sound. Because of she scare. And Kimbop scare too. Some time Smallpock Pang he come in room too much qiet at then on of a sudden you can see he's face like soft moon in picture of Empty Space where rocket it can go but not a man can go unleast he got a suit of Empty Space and ray gun can kill a monstras live at there. On a moon. And on a other plan it they got a monstras too in a movie. Can be thruth. They want a get on we's Earth and eat we because of they is a monstras. And come in dream they always eat at human beans and I got a run hide. But all of a houses can be close and I in a street run hit on door but no can open for Kimbop. They eat a nose then eat a man jab-at-a-girl part so if he no can piss he gone a be died. But in a day time no can see monstras but I can see a Smallpock Pang so I know is thruth of monstras.

Lt. Varga: Washington, I don't think this kid knows anything we want to know. Phone the Koreans and dump him off at the Main Gate.

Kimbop: No-o-o! Mam!

Sgt. Washington: I wonder, ma'am.

Kimbop: No! Mr. Mo he liar at Kimbop! So I trick of he. Say a Police Chief Kang he's daughter she can be Number One baek-boji. But no say she Police Chief daughter. Big trouble at Kimbop now.

Lt. Varga: Baek-boji? What's that?

Sgt. Washington: A woman with no pubic hair, ma'am. No *umoh*. Korean slang. They've got them like that over here. When I was stationed on Oki I heard Japanese men go crazy over them. Spend big bucks. But here on the peninsula they're said to be bad luck.

Lt. Varga: You seem to know a lot about this business, Washington.

Sgt. Washington: My wife's a Korean, ma'am.

Lt. Varga: Oh.

Kimbop: Mam! Mr. Mo liar say King Moonmoo gone a come back Korea kill a bad President Noh Tae Woo and kick Perialist Yankee go home. But No Screaming Baek-boji she say King Moonmoo can be not live Japan.

Just a lie at Kimbop so Kimbop work Mr. Mo he's team point at back-boji so catch she. I believe so at then. Now not. Have a hate at you's Yankee face at then. Now not.

Lt. Varga: Okay, Kimbop. Tell your tale. Anything for better Korean-American relations. Christ!

Kimbop: Because of No Screaming Baek-boji I can know Mr. Mo Tong Lark liar. See! You know all of times we go and catch girl she always gone a cry she scare. And a baek-boji she gone a cry a most because of I don't know. I think she shame of she's pussy am baek-boji no got a hair cover of it shame. But baek-boji she cry a most, of any reason. So on a day at before we catch No Screaming Baek-boji I say Mr. Mo I spy college girl baek-boji house live Gyo-weh-dong. Mr. Mo can think I know baek-bo-ji because of she's face. Kimbop secret. Really bathhouse spy so I know. Mr. Mo no know so. So I and Grabber Lee and Smallpock Pang go out night at then and I say go there Gyo-weh-dong street. All we wait on corner of street she's house. She come home got a pruse in arm and snappy blue skrit is short fashion. I got out a Bongo van and walks at she. *Hello.* She say. Hello. I say. Got a 600 won money for Kimbop? I say. *Why?* She say. Can't got a bus no money home and tired to walk. I say. *Okay.* She say. She's big money house, I see. But not shy of street walking kid. So I gives Smallpock Pang a hi sign in a van he comes easy at girl and I. Grabber Lee big grin of wide. Quick as eels he's arms out a side door van she fall back ways in open door like back over jump of circus guy on tv. And I jumps in and all we go wild around a corner. Grabber Lee he hold baek-boji down floor clutch a mouth so she no scream. Just a eyes moving, no struggle. *What can be this?* Grabber Lee he say. *We got a crazy girl or may be stone of head girl?* But she no talking. Smallpock Pang he take van at factory road at dark of no street lamp. Then Smallpock Pang and Grabber Lee gone a pull down of panty of baek-boji and sure is baek-boji but not right. Because of she no cry. Grabber Lee he put in finger to hole like pull up hook out fish mouth catched and say *Ho this one no chawn-yaw. Ho may be other team catch this one before they throw she back in like a fish catch but too much small.*

Lt. Varga: Chawn-yaw?

Sgt. Washington: Virgin, ma'am.

Lt. Varga: Terrific. I guess I've got some things to learn about this country.

Kimbop: But she no chawn-yaw sure as day am night and Grabber Lee and Smallpock Pang and I looks at a face of each other face and blink a eyes and say *What we gone a do?* Mr. Mo he no want girl she already jab in by man. So I say Can't give such girl King Moonmoo must have chawn-yaw. Grabber Lee and Smallpock Pang say *Shut the mouth.*

Let she go, I say. *Shut the mouth.* They say. Girl look at us calm as a waller melon field under a moon shine. Like she surprise we surprise. Grabber Lee say *Who jab in you, little bitch dog?* But a girl she no talking behind of she's face like hard wall of no posters say nothing. Just stare. Smallpock Pang he can't know of we gone a do of she. He's face gone a think time at then. Mr. Mo he only want chawn-yaw baek-boji give King Moonmoo, not a girl of be jab by man ago. But she pretty in a face and a round buttock of she size. Grabber Lee he smack of she's buttock crack sound. But she no say it can hurted. At then Smallpock Pang start van and go downtown red light street and Grabber Lee he is say *Mr. Mo no want this already jab in girl. So may be we can catch a bonus money sell a No Screaming Baek-boji at common house of whore.* So we do. But I no go in house because of I can't want a sell baek-boji at house of such place. Okay you catch baek-boji ship off King Moonmoo she gone a be happy girl and a woman time she gone a be princess. Umoh chawn-yaw girl she can marry nae-si gone a be okay nae-si no jab in she. Can't. Or Number One baek-boji be a qeen. Have a robe of fur animo and a stick of gold touch a frog gone a be gold man hero soldier. Mr. Mo say. But a No Screaming Baek-boji sell at common house of whore can be not good. Only because of she had jab in by a man like chew already food.

Lt. Varga: Washington, I'm lost. What on God's green earth is a nae-si?

Kimbop: No got a balls man.

Sgt. Washington: There you go.

Lt. Varga: Kimbop, who's this King Munmu? Moon-moo.

Kimbop: King of Korea but not live Korea because of Perialist Yankee love a bad President Noh Tae Woo. So he can live Japan till got big army come back Korea kill bad Noh Tae Woo and kick Yankee go home. Mr. Mo say. But now I no can know. Mr. Mo say King Moonmoo have like big gold barn inside there keep all he's baek-boji. All time they can sit color pillows day long and night time sleep on a gold mattress qiet behind some curtain. Curtain all color green and pruple and red and yellow banana color be design. At a door of gold barn got nae-si guard with wide pants and belt may be have diamond and a hat is towel of Indo like a auntie wear she carry pot on head of she. Nae-si he got none balls because of cut off so no can jab in King Moonmoo he's baek-boji harem.

Sgt. Washington: Lieutenant, can I ask him a question?

Lt. Varga: Be my guest.

Sgt. Washington: Kimbop, you said you can recognize a baek-boji by her *face*?

Lt. Varga: Sergeant!

Kimbop: Kimbop no can. Mr. Mo Tong Lark think a Kimbop can know so. Think a Kimbop clever boy. No stone head of street boy.

Lt. Varga: Washington, dammit! The kid can't be but twelve years old!

Kimbop: Is sure nonebody can know baek-boji by look face. But Mr. Mo he can think Kimbop know so. Because of I say lie at he. Oh is easy, I say like that. Look a fore head got V shape of hair call widow speak English langage. Got a dumple of she's chin. Gone a be baek-boji most time. I say Mr. Mo such kind lie. Or got cat face and sqinch eye most time gone a be baek-boji too. I say like that many thing. But only Kimbop can know she is she is not baek-boji, I say he. Mr. Mo he very like Kimbop speak. Say Kimbop you got born in talent. You catch baek-boji one time week you gone a get bonus money a week. Mr. Mo no can know of how I do. Is secret. I can be veil boy because of I got a be urchint street boy. King Moonmoo come Korea time at then he gone a make Kimbop be a captain because of talent in born I got. Yes. I think at then.

Sgt. Washington: What's your secret, Kimbop?

Kimbop: I can't want a say.

Lt. Varga: That's fine. I don't think we need to know any more.

Kimbop: Okay, I gone a say. Of all. Street boy he can be

like see through. Nonebody can't notice of he. I go people bathhouse. Man bath a door lady bath a other door. I so small boy. But can climb. People bathhouse got a big pipe of air go in go out, make fresh. I go man door pay 2000 won money fee. Make like undress take bath but go pipe of air get climb in up. Can find hole peek of out. Easy. Watch a no clothes womans at wash she's body time. Can get lucky spy baek-boji. Hundred womans may be one can be baek-boji. Old, some time. Too much young, some time. But can be lucky boy. High school girl. College girl. They got there not this time okay next time. Easy see. Easy know. Kimbop can go out side bathhouse. Can wait any time baek-boji come out carry she's shampoo bottle pink placstic dish she use wash time. Go home she. Can follow. Nonebody care of street boy follow. Who he can be? Be nonebody. Follow she she's home. Big house small house can be same. Baek-boji is baek-boji. Then go say Mr. Mo Kimbop know baek-boji she's street live. Slap of back *Good Boy!* he say like that. Then a night Smallpock Pang and Grabber Lee we go in Bongo. Wait front side house at a corner she's street. Gate can open she come out side may be go store buy a milk or popsuckle summer time. Then we catch. More one for King Moonmoo he's delight. Mr. Mo he no can know of bathhouse climb way. Got a be secret. So King Moonmoo he gone a make Kimbop captain help kick Perialist Yankee go home. You. I believe so at then. Now not. Gone a hate you's face at then. Now not. Mr. Mo Tong Lark liar. Sell baek-boji Japan business man big money. I find out a night Smallpock Pang try cutted off Kimbop's balls make Kimbop nae-si.

Sgt. Washington: What on earth happened, Kimbop?

Kimbop: Smallpock Pang and Grabber Lee a night drink too much bottles soju alcol. Gone a be heh-leh-leh. Gone a be drunk. They talky I talky. Ask a Smallpock Pang say King Moonmoo come back Korea time story. When come? I say. *You crazy boy.* He say. Soon? I say. *You crazy boy talk King Moonmoo talk nae-si talk baek-boji harem bullshit.* He say like that. Not crazy. I say. Is thruth. You can be drunk man. I say like that. *I show you nae-si.* He say. *Come here monkey boy.* Smallpock Pang he got a jack knife. Grabber Lee he grab Kimbop pull down a pants at ankle I struggles. Let me go! Go! Smallpock Pang he a Kimbop knife blade stick out switch back switch back I hear a air so close sound. Smallpock Pang take a leg hold up high I jumpy one foot hop say NO! NO! Smallpock Pang he reach touch I close a eyes all a water of tears drubble out. Stop you Son Of A Bitch I gone a need it for be man some days. But Kimbop no can be see only in a brain can see fish dead eye. Can't know why but see fish dead eye at bottom a well water cold. *Ha ha* Smallpock Pang and Grabber

Lee got a laugh then unlease me I got a run a pants at a ankle like wild animo bited won't let Kimbop be go. Runned, Kimbop. Runned. Kimbop breath say Run Kimbop a Run Don't Stop Now Ever.

Lt. Varga: Jesus, kid.

Kimbop: But where a boy gone a run? Just go blind walk one hour time. Kimbop be nonebody can go no where. So by and by can be at red light street bottom of hill. House of whore hill. Some kind power pull Kimbop at there. I thinks now. Pass all a windows of womans in honey moon hanbok dress color shine of old days court lady. Nonebody can see of Kimbop because of I only urchint of street. Come at house of whore we sell No Screaming Baek-boji. She can be sit watch tv drama other whore womans sit too. Then she see Kimbop at a window look in start a cry but not make of tear because of she's face powder red lip. But a eyes say. I make a finger mouth sign Shush I got a talk you. Mama-san she see of me *Scat! Monkeyhead!* So I can go in alley climb of window bars up. And in of toilet room. Can be good climb boy. Kimbop. Crul up in side small closet of towel wait. By and by she come up of steps. No Screaming Baek-boji and drunk man of not Korean. She talk a soft. Then grunt time in room. Next she come in toilet room because of hose of hole wash. Now I got say. She can of jump like see rat more big than dog. But

I say of Shush again. *What you want to me?* She say. I got know. I say. *What?* She say. You been Japan? I say. *Japan man like baek-boji. Like a look stare at she's boji. Gentleman clean but make a girl shake of heart.* She say like that. You see of King Moonmoo? I say. *What?* She say. He gone a come Korea make reunificated and free of no Perialist Yankee go home. I say. He got a barn of gold Japan keep of baek-boji princess and qeen and a nae-si guard. Is thruth? I got a know thruth. I say like that. *You crazy boy. Moon-moo King he of die five hundred year. You got a head rot, boy.* She say. No. I say. Mr. Mo Tong Lark he say me like that. King Moonmoo got a army nae-si sword and wide col-or pant. Come Korea kill of bad President Noh Tae Woo and Yankee go home we can be free of. Say thruth. I say like that. *Ha!* She say and teeth smile wide of white. *Ha!* Again. Then I not say of anything. Maybe she can lie no go at Japan never. She look Kimbop funny kind of look at. Like may be I excape Spirit House no got a brain. Why you no scream we catch you in Bongo time? I say like that. You crazy you no scream. Anybody baek-boji she gone a howl like of dog bloodjun up for eat dog meat soup. You no scream. Why? I say like that. *First time Bongo I scream. I cratch a nail finger at grabber man. He hitted of me. Hardly. More hardly. Then Japan boat next day. No I can do else. So why I scream Bongo second time? Same again thing gone a be.* She say like that. At then Kimbop can know of all. King Moonmoo no can be. Nae-si no can be. Only ago time. Baek-boji can be but only Japan rich man have she.

Lt. Varga: Kimbop, why did you sneak onto the base this morning?

Kimbop: Because of I say already you. Mr. Mo Tong Lark can be liar at Kimbop. So I gone a trick he and get put jail place he. A before time I spy a baek-boji young girl of high school. Pretty. In bathhouse wash she's body easy slow. Eye bright sprackle. Too much pretty girl. May be King Moonmoo qeen she's woman time. Follow she she's house. Big house of Police Chief Kang everybody know. No tell Mr. Mo. Girl she can be too much pretty Kimbop no can want Grabber Lee Smallpock Pang touch she's boji. Even only test she can be chawn-yaw not chawn-yaw. Kimbop no can want a do so of she. I thinks King Moonmoo come a Korea can have wedding feast time of she. Best wait. I can thinks. But King Moonmoo is not be. Only Mr. Mo liar say. So I do a evil. Like a monstras. Say I see a baek-boji million dollar girl. No spot of she. And is thruth. Ask Mr. Mo big bonus money this girl. Too much pretty. I say Mr. Mo. He say *Kimbop you got eye of devil in Hell. She can be Number One baek-boji I gives you bonus money two times. Get she.* So we do. Grabber Lee and Smallpock Pang van park corner pretty baek-boji she's school. Only Kimbop know she can be Police Chief he's baby. No can want a say now about catch she. Cry so much in van clamspse she's wrist and ankles hurt. Grabber Lee pull down a panties stuff she's mouth qiet. I say you before like this. She's eyes I no can say of. Like got died. Mr. Mo big trouble now. Police Chief he gone a know now. He's baby she's boji got jab in by Grabber Lee a finger. Too much pretty girl. Police Chief gone a get Mr. Mo Tong Lark. Mr. Mo gone a get Kimbop. Perialist Yankee no gone a be kick go home. King Moonmoo no can know because of be died five hundred year. So I come American soldier place you can help Kimbop. Only I think.

Lt. Varga: Sergeant.

Sgt. Washington: Ma'am?

Lt. Varga: Take him out the back gate.

Sgt. Washington: And let him go?

Lt. Varga: And, Sergeant.

Sgt. Washington: Ma'am?

Lt. Varga: Have somebody from Maintenance cut that tree down.

By the time the album of polaroid snapshots reached Rookie Patrolman Pak it had already passed through the hands of everyone above him in his Section and more than half a dozen of the fifty-odd photos had disappeared. This did not surprise Rookie Patrolman Pak. Some of the snapshots were said to be "better" than the others. The poses, of course, were pretty much the same: the young woman in each lay sprawled on the back seat of the taxi, her skirt or dress hiked above her waist, her panties gone, her legs spread wide enough to reveal the wet pink of a violated cleft, her face puffy but relaxed with the zoned-out look of the drugged and the occasional thread of drool oozing from the corner of her mouth. In the instances where she had worn slacks or jeans, these were gone too.

Some of the young women were prettier than the others and Rookie Patrolman Pak figured that the very prettiest ones were also the missing ones. This only made sense. He wondered if he dare take one for himself, but as a mere Rookie Patrolman this did not seem wise. He should be grateful Detective Lt. Ko had said to Evidence Clerk Lee, "Let Pak have a look at them. Let him have a look at what goes on out there at night. Let him head straight for the

Men's Room–then he'll do one of two things, eh? Ha ha!"
Rookie Patrolman Pak turned the stiff leaves of the album
with its four polaroid snapshots per page carefully cen-
tered in their quadrants. The taxi driver had snapped each
one from the same angle so that the private part of the
young woman came out clear and well-defined, though
the faces on the tilted-back heads of some of the young
women were beyond identification. If you woke up out of
a drugged stupor and a man leaned over you and shoved a
photo in front of your nose and said "This is your face and
your filthy *boji* and if you tell anyone about tonight you
know what you can expect from me"–well, what would a
decent girl do? She would not broadcast her degradation
and heap more shame upon herself. It was, Rookie Patrolman Pak reflected, unfair. But the young woman was not
without her involvement in the affair. This kind of thing
didn't happen in broad daylight. These young women had
been out late. Past 10 PM. And some of the skirts weren't
so long they needed a lot help getting above her hips. And
didn't common sense dictate you don't accept a stick of
gum–or any kind of tasty drink or wrapped sweet–from
a stranger? Korean women were too trusting and polite.
They treat everybody they meet like part of one big family, and that's not the way life is.

Rookie Patrolman Pak turned the stiff leaves of the al-

bum. Four girls per page. Four puffy faces. Four black tufts
and four slivers of pink. In between, a rumpled sweater
or a disheveled blouse and a skirt turned inside-out. As
different as each face was in its way–one young woman
seemed almost to be smiling coyly and another seemed in
the throes of a religious experience and a third seemed to
be sneaking a supercilious peek at the action–they were
all the same for all that. Until he came to the seventh
page, top right. Here he paused, uncertain, lingering over
the parted lips, the slack chin. The dilated, round nostrils. He could almost feel them breathing. But with the
head thrown back in this particular snapshot, the eyes,
the browridge, the forehead were almost beyond ken, like
a dim landscape on the edge of a horizon. But the girl's
pubic triangle–an elongated, slender wedge of maidenish
hairs like a narrowing phalanx of ants disappearing into
a crevice nicked in pallid flesh–stunned him.

*

Only a Korean man, the American thought as he read
the morning newspaper spread out in front of him on the
kitchen table, would rape a woman and then drive her
home and leave her with his telephone number. It was
all there in an article framed by ads for English language

institutes and satellite tv services and headhunting agencies. How the college girl had jumped to her death from the fourteenth floor of her apartment building. How her mother had found her diary and read it and how the girl had transcribed the taxi driver's phone number in red felt-tip pen at the end of the final entry. How the mother had carried the diary to the police station the day after the funeral. How the police had picked up the cabby and opened his trunk and found the photo album of polaroid snapshots. Fifty young women. Over fifty. Fifty-two, to be exact. How the police had gone over the cab and found fifty-two identical slashes carved in the driver's leather steering wheel cover. "Handle," they call it, instead of steering wheel, which was appropriate enough, given how the locals just seem to just grab on to the thing and hold on for dear life.

The American clipped the article from the page, folded it twice and tucked it in his pocket. He needed a topic for the morning's Advanced English Conversation class. They had been through everything in the textbook from UFO Abductions through Abortion and Asian Women's Preference for Sons during the first half of the term and he was feeling pressed to come up something "fresh." This might bedevil the consciences of the students enough to last a whole class period. Maybe two, if he could coax the girl with the glittery black eyes and high, tight butt–a rare sight in Asia!—to open up a little. It was the sullenness of the pretty ones that bothered him. He didn't much care anymore if the Plain Janes jumped in or not. Or if the males like the one who called himself Muammar even bothered to show up at all. Though inevitably they did, along with the jabbering, irrepressible homely girls with the Minnie Mouse pencil boxes and Brad Pitt book covers.

The American had an arithmetical figure he tossed about in his mind as he showered after reading reports like this one in the morning paper. In his twenty-six years of life in the States and one in Mexico, he had known personally only three women who confessed to him they had been raped. And one of these was possibly the most lascivious drunk he had ever met in his life. In three years in Seoul, fully seven women had come out and told him they had been violated by strangers or men they knew. Eight, if you counted Hee-jung and the Dutch woman missionary. The American sometimes wondered if there weren't something in his character, some subtle display of empathy operating on a level he was unaware of, that eased the delivery of such confidences. Back in the States he had rarely thought about rape, except on special consciousness-raising campus occasions like Take Back the Night night. In Korea he thought about it almost every day–especially in the mornings. He wondered sometimes, in those morning moments of honesty so airy and fleeting they seldom left even the remotest tracings of an imprint, if he was becoming more perverse, more sensitive, or merely more angry. Or all three at once, though that scarcely seemed possible.

After stuffing his lunchtime sandwiches into his briefcase and checking his watch, he sat down at the typewriter and knocked out a quick one:

LIKE PISTOL GRIPS: MACHISMO
KOREAN STYLE: SEOUL

Young women are cautioned against
accepting anything to eat or drink
from taxi drivers, particularly after
sunset, as these offerings are often
laced with drugs.
—News Report

When they uncrumpled
his totaled
taxi
and removed the headless
corpse

and pried open the buckled
trunk
they found a polaroid
snapshot album
of his victims' spread
crotches
which they checked against
what they'd found
carved into
the steering wheel:
fifty-two identical
notches

The "crotches/notches" rhyme was just right, he decided as he typed up a clean copy with someone special
in mind, in the end resisting the impulse to overcorrect
himself with "gashes/slashes." It wasn't Shakespeare, he
knew, or Keats or even cummings, but they didn't have 10
AM classes.

*

Taxidriver Baek had neither the time, the money, nor
the inclination for whores. He has fathered two children,
a son, seventeen, and a thirteen-year-old daughter. His

wife aborted a third child, a female. He has been driving a taxi for nine years, ever since his brother-in-law, six
years his senior, went bankrupt. His brother-in-law had
had a shop producing counterfeit Izod labels that were
stitched on sport shirts that were sold to Western tourists and American GIs in Itaewon, a tourist area in Seoul
known for its bargains and hookers. Business was good
because the labels were good, even better than the real
thing, his brother-in-law had pointed out just before a foreign government raised such a stink and the Ministry of
Justice was forced to raid a couple of the smaller operations. Taxidriver Baek was his brother-in-law's hands-on
man just as the business was swinging into full swing.
Nudged off the swing he fell plumb into the driver's seat
of a company cab and discovered a vocation. Within four
years he had a cab of his own and no one to answer to,
except Bin-hee, his wife.

The police had succeeded in locating taxidriver Baek
because taxidriver Baek had left his phone number and a
note in the purse of his last rape victim before he let her
off, no doubt groggy and bit wobbly in the knees, in front
of her apartment building. Identifying the other fifty-one
victims would not prove so easy because taxidriver Baek
had trained the lens of his polaroid camera more on the
naked crotches than on the faces of the women. Neverthe-

less, taxidriver Baek had left notes threatening to expose at least fourteen of his victims' degradations unless they paid him one million *won* (about $900) in "security money." This was known because taxi-driver Baek had left a notebook underneath the photo album listing the names and addresses of these fourteen victims, and when and where they had met him for the pay-offs and how much they had coughed up. It was not known whether any or all of the other thirty-seven victims had received such notes, whether or not they had contacted him or if any payments had been made. Of the fourteen victims whose names and addresses were known from the notebook, seven denied that they had ever been raped and, when shown photos of their puffy, zoned-out faces, contended that "Many women look like that. That's not me (or mine)." Five others admitted under interrogation that they had been violated in the manner outlined above and had made at least one pay-off, one woman having stated she had given taxidriver Baek a total of four million *won* (about $3600) in "hush money" on four separate occasions. A sixth victim whose name and address were known had committed suicide, but the exact circumstances surrounding the tragedy were unclear. The seventh victim had left the Republic and was living overseas, presumably in the United States or Canada.

Detective Lt. Ko, at a meeting with three of the city's senior detectives and with the photo album spread open on the top of his desk, asked for suggestions and watched three pairs of shoulders rise and fall in a single shrug. Though he had been able to match the names of all fourteen of the women in taxidriver Baek's notebook with photos and though the last photo in the album clearly belonged to the suicide whose diary entry had exposed the monster in the first place (a photo ceremoniously and mercifully burned at the bottom of a metal wastebasket late one evening by a revolted Detective Lt. Ko himself), still he hadn't been able to pin a name on a single one of the remaining victims, and Deputy Chief Choi–his immediate supervisor–had insinuated just the day before that perhaps Detective Lt. Ko was losing his touch. Detective Lt. Ko had even convinced Precinct Captain Ku to offer ten promotion points to anyone who could crack an i.d. on even just one of the "unknowns" but the offer had to be rescinded when a neighborhood housewives' council complained about patrolmen canvassing local market stalls and distracting rapt, chin-scratching male merchants from hawking their genuine sneakers and sportswear. When the story finally hit the newspapers, it did so with a vengeance and city crime reporters, bristling at being kept in the dark for so long but agreeing not to print any given names, wanted ages, marital statuses, occupations, and family names–this last no serious breach of privacy in a country where better than two-fifths of the population share the surnames Kim, Pak, or Lee–to flesh out their articles. The snapshots of the fourteen women who had been identified had been checked off with a black felt-tip pen, but Detective Lt. Ko still had photos of twenty-nine (eight had long before disappeared from the album, like gap-teeth in one long paginated death grin) young women on his hands and no idea of what their names were, to say nothing about how to locate them. These twenty-nine anonymous snapshots had become so familiar to Detective Lt. Ko and the others in the precinct station that many of them now went by shamelessly vulgar "nicknames"–the inventions of rakish bachelor Sergeant Lim and Evidence Clerk Lee–rather than case numbers: postage stamp, horned caduceus, maidenhair fern, brushfire, peek-a-boo, forked pennant, shaggy lady, black-beetles-swarm-the-honey-pot, etc.

Some minutes after Detective Lt. Ko ushered his three senior colleagues from his office, Rookie Patrolman Pak approached uncertainly the pebbled glass of this same office door and, choking back a frothy mixture of revulsion and shame rising in his throat, decided not to go in and speak about what he knew after all.

The gloom of the overcast, drizzly late autumn morning seemed to have soaked into the very souls of the students, who sat listlessly in their desk-chairs and gazed up at the American with what Koreans call *myung-tae nun*—"dead pollack eyes." Morning receptions like this present a special challenge to a teacher who needs the cooperation, if not the bubbling enthusiasm, of the entire group, but this morning the American felt he was up to it. After dutifully taking roll by calling out the given names—"Esther" "John" "Peter" "Madonna"—he had instructed his charges to choose for themselves on the very first day of class, he passed out copies of the article he had clipped from the newspaper only an hour earlier. The usual murmurs of confusion and muted alarm rippled through the classroom as when any novelty was introduced into the routine—today clearly they were going to be denied the security blanket of a textbook lesson format—and the American knew how adroitly he launched into the topic would determine how successfully the hour would go. He opted for the "personal" approach he had been turning over in his mind in those minutes he spent trundling up the steps of the Foreign Languages Building.

"This morning, after reading the English-language

newspaper," he announced as darkly and meaningfully as he could, "I wrote a poem. It wasn't a very good poem, I guess. But in my rush to get ready for class, I still felt a powerful compulsion to express myself. And so I sat down and wrote it. Now together let's read the article that so affected me and see how it affects you."

At this point he scanned the room of faces, searching for the pair of glittery black eyes that belonged to Lily, she of the high, tight butt and competent English. He wanted her to know that he wrote poems. That he was more than a knock-off of Mr. Ed The Magical English-Speaking Horse with a pedagogical twist, though he would not have minded if she imagined that he was hung with such equine splendor. When he finally located her–she was sitting to his right near a window today, having moved up and back and sideways like a *Through the Looking Glass* chess piece throughout the first half-semester–he called on her to read the first sentence of the article.

"Yesterday a Seoul taxi driver," she began haltingly, "was arrested on charges of raping as many as 52 high school and college students and young housewives over a period of five years."

The girl was visibly moved and her black eyes ceased to glitter as she struggled to get the last words out. The American remembered an English literature professor who years before had induced in him the same suffocating shortness of breath–what Koreans call *dahp-dahp hada*–whenever he was required to read a Herbert or Donne poem aloud in the classroom, and he rebuked himself for putting the poor girl through the ordeal.

"Thank you, Lily. Your pronunciation is improving. There were ten 'r' sounds and three 'l' sounds in that sentence, and you misfired on only two of them. Keep it up," he encouraged her, wondering apropos of nothing if she would be able to pronounce the difference between "leer" and "rear" and making a mental note to construct a naughty tongue-twister around "A li'l leer at Lily's really rare rear" when he had the time. Humbert Humbert, he preened, you ain't got nothing on this guy.

"Now, Muammar," he nodded to the ardent nationalist student activist with rabbit teeth who was convinced that homosexuality had been introduced into his country by American GIs at the nearby military base (or else by the CIA, it depended) with the intention of "softening steely Korean manhood to putty" and making the peninsula easier to exploit as a vassal state. "Would you please read the next sentence."

Muammar scrutinized the sheet of paper in front of him as if he were deconstructing the text for some treacherous hidden meaning and, failing to find the unfairly privileged half of a fatal binary opposition, obeyed. "Baek Bum-nok, 42, of Itaewon-dong, Yongsan-gu, was apprehended only after the mother of his latest victim brought her daughter's diary to the attention of . ."

*

Of the five females who acknowledged they had been raped by taxidriver Baek and who agreed to press charges against him, the testimony of Kim Mi-ryong (not her real name), 28, is fairly representative: "He picked me up in front of Seoul (Train) Station. I had just arrived from Tae-gu and was a little tired from the journey, so I was very happy to catch a taxi so quickly. I decided not to stand in line at the Taxi Queue because you can wait there for an hour in the blowing rain on some days. I decided to take my chances by walking down the street a ways and hailing a taxi from there. That's where he picked me up—not in front of the station exactly. He seemed like a very nice man, like an older brother. Clean-shaven and soft-spoken and very personable and not like some taxi drivers who stink of soju, you know, and his taxi was spotless inside too. I could tell he took good care of it. I was a little tired because I had had to take the Bidulgi (cheap) train and not the Saemaul Express from Taegu and the trip took six

68

hours with so many stops. I told him to take me to Bong-sang-dong, which is where my sister and brother-in-law live and whom I had been staying with while I searched for an apartment of my own in Seoul. Because I'm originally from Taegu and only just recently had gotten a job in Seoul. He seemed very nice, like I said, and didn't grumble when I told him where I wanted to go, Bongsang-dong. Because some taxi drivers don't like to go there because it's outside of town a bit and not so populous and sometimes they complain that they won't be able to find a return fare and sometimes try to charge you extra because of this. He offered me a Yakult–the yogurt drink that comes in the little throw-away plastic bottle with the silver-paper cap. I drank it through the little plastic straw that he gave me that comes with the Yakult. I was already tired and didn't think about it when I became woozy and then I passed out. When I woke up . . . I was in the back seat still but lying on my back. My skirt was above my hips and I don't know what happened to my underpanties. But, no, I didn't realize that at first because I was still groggy and for a moment thought I was still on the train from Taegu. Then I focused my eyes and saw him leaning over the front seat and looking down at me. First at my face and then at my, you know, down-below. He was smiling. He asked me how much money I made a month. (I had already told him my job earlier when we had a conversation.) At first I didn't understand anything and then I began to know that something terrible had happened. My down-below felt cold and so I put my hands down there and I discovered I was naked and he could see everything and so quickly I pulled down my skirt and tried to sit up. But he pushed me back down and told me to lie still. Then he showed me the picture. The photograph snapshot. He held it in front of my eyes but wouldn't let me touch it when I tried to grab it from him. I had no quickness still and couldn't get it. And he was strong, too. I knew this when he pushed me down. He asked me how much money I made a month again and then he wanted to know my phone number too. I refused to say anything. What could I say? What could I do? It was hard to think. It was impossible to think. Then he said some truly disgusting things that I will not repeat here, though I remember them just as clearly as if it were this morning. Nobody in my life had ever spoken that way in front of me. I felt like a cheap whore. So he drove me home–I mean to my sister's apartment building. I was crying now, but I noticed that his taxidriver's permit on the dashboard was gone–if it had been there in the first place, I don't know. I got out of the taxi. I just wanted to get away from that disgusting, horrible man. My sister and brother-in-law were asleep when I got inside the apartment. I had been staying with them for two months and I had a key. I went into the bathroom and washed every part of my body, for every part of me felt soiled in a way. Then I went to bed and tried to sleep but I could only cry silently. I didn't want anybody to wake up and find out what had happened. The next morning I opened my purse and saw that he had taken all my money too. And he had left a note in my purse with his phone number on it and some threatening words about the photograph. I kept thinking about the photograph for weeks. Finally I called the number and asked him what he wanted. He wanted money. So I met him and paid him one million *won.* That was one month's salary, and part of the money I had put aside for apartment key money. I thought he would give me the photograph then. But he didn't. He just disappeared with my money. Foolishly I had given him my phone number at that meeting. Because I thought he was going to give me the photograph. And then I could be done with him. But he didn't give it to me. He called me twice more, but I never met him again. I knew he would never give me the photograph. Sometimes I wondered if there had ever really been a photograph. I was drugged, you know, when he showed it to me. So I just refused to speak to him. I just hung up when he called. That was two years ago. That's all I want to say. Isn't that all I have to say?"

Rookie Patrolman Pak decided to become a policeman sometime during the protracted funk he suffered after being dumped by Young-hee, the girl he had dated without her parents' knowledge during the two years after high school while he hung about looking for a job and waiting, with fatalistic equanimity, for his military induction notice. Up to two years of military service is compulsory in the Republic of South Korea and though few young men look forward to it, fewer still dare express any apprehension about its notorious rigors. All he hoped was that he would not be stationed along the DMZ and have to stay up on guard duty the long winter nights staring into the frozen north and listening to the incessant propaganda harangues broadcast over loudspeakers by the government of the Democratic People's Republic of North Korea.

The night before he was to report for his physical examination, he took Young-hee to a *yogwan*–a modest inn frequented by lovers, penurious travelers, and streetwalkers and their johns–and they made love for the first time. It was the first time he had seen her naked–indeed the first time he had seen *any* woman unclothed. And naturally enough her body was a marvel. He adored her breasts and said so. When she got up off the *yo*–a sort of heavy quilt serving as a mattress on the floor of the *yogwan* room—to use the toilet, he had to stifle the urge to hoot in exclaim at the supple animal movement and shapeliness of her rounded, low-slung buttocks as she crossed the room. But most resplendent of all on that first night of lovemaking was the configuration of her pubic tuft: like a phalanx of black ants narrowing to a point and then disappearing into a tiny cleft nicked in her flesh. But he felt no urge to cry aloud at this revelation as Young-hee entered the room again and crossed the floor toward him and settled at his side. For he understood that she was sharing with him that night a deep and private secret that mere praise could never hope to do justice. And, besides that, there was the simple fact that his breath had been completely taken away.

Private Pak received his Dear John letter only days before he was to go on leave for the Lunar New Year's holidays, three days of gorging on his mother's food and binge drinking with his old high school classmates. And, until he opened Young-hee's short, hand-scrawled note and read her awkward, strangely stilted argument why she felt they were longer "compatible," at least one night of love. Back home, he tried ringing her up half a dozen times the first day, but her mother's curt *Eupsuh!* ("Not here!") each time left him standing alone in the phone booth feeling foolish, abused, and resentful. The mother had never liked him—he wasn't college-bound—and it clearly made no difference that he was now serving their country.

He asked his friends—their dating was no secret among his peers—if they had seen her, but by all accounts it was if she had been swept off the face of the earth. Koreans' is a "face-saving" culture and not unusually does the jilting partner of a pair seem to simply disappear rather than confront the complicated linguistic matter of saying, politely and respectfully, "I just don't care for you the way I used to." One friend took him aside the afternoon of the day before he was to return to his unit and intimated that he had heard that somebody had spotted Young-hee working in a none too savory place. And plying a none too savory trade. Private Pak could tell that this friend had more information than he was letting on and pressed him with all the considerable urgency a young man in uniform and on military leave can muster. She was working in an area called Texas Alley in a bar called Injun Joe's, a hangout for horny American GIs with too many dollars and too much empty bedtime on their hands.

That any of this might be true haunted the rest of Private Pak's afternoon and early evening with hurtful, maddening insistence. He knew that he had to verify the rumor and, if true, confront her with his rage and indignation. That a young woman with Young-hee's spirit and good looks and decent prospects might choose to become a whore was incredible, but such a woman whoring for foreigners was wholly unthinkable, a gross violation of everything good and true. So when he strode in mufti into Injun Joe's and saw her sitting in a booth in the smoky half-light between two huge American GIs, he doubted that it was really her at all. And when her eyes drifted across the room and fell upon his stunned gaze, they showed no sign of recognition. Instead in them smoldered the contempt that he knew such women—women who had gone to bed with foreigners for money—felt for the men of her own people. She saw him not as a man, an individual, her former lover, but as a damning accusatory finger pointing from a panel of those righteous ghost judges in the old stories. He saw this in her eyes and knew that this was not her, not really her, and turned and walked away. He could not save her. She was too far gone. She was not herself anymore.

*

The class had come off rather well, the American thought, despite the shaky start. Lily and Muammar said nothing further during the entire period, but the others—

especially the homely girls with their plump cheeks and enjambed dentition—had picked up the slack with alacrity. Most everyone had an opinion on the college student's suicide, and these opinions, like votes, slipped evenly and neatly into two opposing slots. Some felt that she had no choice but to kill herself, as horrible as it sounded to say that. The memory of the violation would haunt her to the end of her days. And the knowledge that the vile monster had her photograph would just make the affair all that much more unbearable. It could surface at any time. What if someone robbed the taxi driver's taxi and made off with the pictures and published them in some underground dirty magazine? Pornography was on the rise and lapping at people's heels like a backed up sewer and Confucian Korea could do little to staunch the flow. What if the taxi driver had an accident and was knocked unconscious or killed and the rescue workers came across the snapshot album? (At this suggestion the American drew back a moment and pressed his shoulder blades against the blackboard and wondered if the girl called Eureka had somehow stumbled upon access to his darkest fantasies.) What if she got lucky and married a successful man and the taxi driver tracked her down and blackmailed her the way he had some of the other women? There simply would be no end to her misery. She had to die.

Others felt her life could have been salvaged. Suicide is never an acceptable solution. With counseling. The help of her family and friends. People were more open-minded and understanding these days. Some good man might even marry her. She wasn't ruined. Any psychological hurt can be repaired. Any disgrace. It takes time, sure. Buddhist nunneries were full of recovering women, and some of them even returned to "social life." And she had the son-of-a-bitch's (one female student actually used the word, *gaeseki*) phone number. The police, the legal system, a long stretch in the penitentiary. If she had been a close friend of mine, the student named Richard boasted in an English bristling with unnuanced thrusts in just about every direction, I would have found the bastard out and cut off his–here he fumbled for just the right word–"janitor." (Presumably, the American hazarded, he meant "genitals.") The American noted that it was the students who most believed in the infinite possibilities of redemption who employed the foulest language, and wondered if he might be missing something.

Yes, the American thought, the class had come off well. Almost every one had seized upon the opportunity to get their English out into the open air–well, anyway, the classroom was hardly hermetically insulated–and give it some exercise. And, better, later that afternoon Lily showed up at his office door. He invited her in and she sat down in the wooden desk-chair that student visitors inevitably chose as proper to their station. In her hands she clutched the sheet of paper he had folded twice and tucked into her palm in the hallway after class. It had been a rather daring thing to do, he knew, but she was a couple years older than the other sophomores and didn't seem to share confidences with her classmates. He had been watching her for better than six weeks now. Those glittery black eyes. That high, tight butt. Her competent English.

"Why did you give me this poem? I don't like this poem. I don't want to read this poem."

"You don't like poetry? But I always see you with books of poetry among your textbooks. I thought you liked poetry."

"I like *real* poetry. Elizabeth Browning. William Yeats. Not this." And in a spasm of befuddled haste she handed him back the sheet of paper folded several more times than the original quarto he had slipped her. "Not this. This is disgusting."

"I'm sorry," he retreated. "I miscalculated. I guess I misguessed."

"Misguessed?"

"A nonce word. A neologism. Again, I'm sorry."

"No. You are a teacher. You shouldn't apologize."

"What else can I do?"

"Explain. Just explain."

"Explain?"

"Yes."

"Well," he struggled for the exact word, the one that would tip the balance, or at least open up an avenue of escape. "I wanted you to understand my anger. My *rage*."

"No. Explain."

"Explain?"

"Yes. Why *me*?"

He thought: Those glittery black eyes. That high, tight butt. Her competent English. And said:

"I just thought you were interested in poetry."

"No. Not like that," she said with grim finality.

"I see."

"Sir?"

"Yes?"

"May I leave now?"

"Yes. Of course. You're free to go any time you wish."

She stood up from the desk-chair and walked to the door. At the door she turned and faced him.

"Sir."

"Yes?"

"I used to think you were cute. Now I think you're a

pig. 'Leda and the Swan' is a beautiful poem because it was a swan. A god. Not a man. Not everyone thinks rape is a joke."

"A joke?"

"Good-bye."

As she exited the room, the American glimpsed the student named Muammar standing in the hall. He waited for a knock on the door, but none came.

*

Rookie Patrolman Pak stood uncertainly outside Detective Lt. Ko's office. This time he knocked on the door and waited for the expected grunt of permission to enter. Then he heard it. And so entered. Stood at attention. Snappily saluted his superior who sat behind his desk turning over the stiff leaves of the photo album.

"Well?"

"Sir, I .."

"Yes, yes. Come one. Which one do you want?"

"Sir?"

"Everybody seems to want a souvenir. You might as well have one too."

"Sir, there is one victim I want to id—"

"So you do have a favorite? So you're no different from

all the others. Well, come on, then. Hurry up."

"Sir, I—"

"Take any one that suits your fancy. We have enough testimony and hard evidence to put this *gaeseki* away for a long, long time."

"Sir—"

"Come on, Pak! You're trying my patience."

"Page seven, sir," he said hurriedly, with all the unthinking obedience of the newcomer to a hierarchy. "Upper right-hand corner."

"That one? You can't see her face at all."

"No, sir. I don't need to," Rookie Patrolman Pak said bitterly as Detective Lt. Ko peeled the snapshot off the adhesive backing of the photo album page and sailed it across his desk like a dealt card.

"I see their faces every night before I go to sleep," Detective Lt. Ko confessed wearily. "Even the faces that are not in the pictures."

"Sir?"

"Tell me, Rookie Patrolman Pak. Can you *imagine* the face of the woman in that picture you chose?"

"No, sir," Rookie Patrolman Pak lied, burying the secret deep and forever in his heart and suddenly feeling all the stronger for it, all the more in control of himself. "I can't imagine her face at all."

"That's very sad, Rookie Patrolman Pak. That's very sad indeed."

"Sir, can—"

"Sorry. Only one to a customer. And remember your place."

"Yes, sir."

"Good. Dismissed."

*

When the American unfolded the sheet of paper that the student named Lily had returned to him, he discovered that it did not contain his poem at all. In its place he found the words of the "declaration" that student protesters had been passing out to everyone at the campus main gate since the big announcement two weeks before. And in spite of—or was it in fact because of?—the execrable grammar and puerile demoniolect of fevered hissing and spitting, he felt the genuine poetry of resentment and pent-up rage leaking through:

NO MORE PLUNDER, YANKEE!

We are giving a strict warning to you just in time of your Bush's coming visit to Korea.

The history of U.S. concerning Korea began with invasions and plunderings, the history of Korea against U.S. was studded with resistances. In Korea war, the sin of your avarice, the U.S.-made bombs killed the Korean people innumerably and miserably. We never forget even a moment the fact that we must revenge on you. You guys have plundered the South Korea as half a colony in many ways after you were frustrated by the North Korea in your plan to make Korea one of your faithful colonies.

The Korean peasants, bereft of all their hope of livelihood by enforced U.S. rice importation, are sharpening the blade of their scythes aimed at your chests. The Korean labors, falling to the floor fatigued with the long-hour working, bear a wish to put your heads into the press. The Korean industrialists of small and medium-sized enterprises, deprived of means of survival, want to burn you guys together with U.S.-made products. And the Korean soldiers, driven to the frontline acting as buletproofs in your futile war game, are about to fire U.S.-made M-16 rifles pointed at your craniums.

Don't be happy with your Bush's coming! Ko-

*rean people are just waiting for your Bush's foot-
steps on Korea with burning hatred. He shall not
be able to stay any moment in this country and
neither will you guys. You will never sleep a wink,
lying on your backs. At any time, at any places –
in your bedroom, in your car, street, lavatory and
restaurant, you will be rightly punished by our
angry iron-fists. We warn you. No more plunder!
Yankees go home together with your troops. This
is the only way your safety is ensured.*

Seoul. The Korean National Democratic Front.

THE JOKE STORY
CAVE

"You awake?" I say.

"Okay."

"Nice butt."

"Humm."

"Look at the crack on you."

"What?"

"It barely comes up to your coccyx."

"Cock-sicks? Don't know cock-sicks."

"Your tailbone. The crack of your butt just barely comes up to your tailbone."

"Same-same crack everybody else."

"No way. It's lower on you. Look."

"You crazy. Anybody can't see own butt. No got turn around head like Exercise lady."

"Exorcist lady."

"Oh."

"You want me to get a mirror?"

"No! Why anybody want a see own *ung-dung-ee*?"

"Well, look at mine then."

"Ugh! Don't show me white man hair butt in a morning!"

"I just want you to see the difference."

"Ugh! You got one *byo-roo-jee.*"

"One what?"

"*Byo-roo-jee.* I don't know English. Jit?"

"A zit."

"Okay."

"Hey. Be careful."

"Fat one."

"Hey, I'm human. What the hell. Ouch!"

"Bloody."

"OW!"

"Sorry. No white stuff. Only blood. You go herb doctor. Give you some medicines."

"That hurt, Ae-jin."

"Not my name."

"Sure it is."

"My name Ae-*joo.*"

"Sorry."

"You no remember Ae-joo name? You too much drinky last night Puss 'n' Booze Club."

"Sure I remember. You're *My name Ae-joo. You buy me whiskey coke. Only ten thousand won.*"

"Not funny."

"Maybe not. But I see a big smile right here in front of me. Just look at the crack of your butt. It's like a big round Happy Face."

"Hey! Why you kiss a butt?"

"I'm a sick man, Ae-joo."

"So you kiss Ae-joo *ung-dung-ee*?"

"It's the only cure. The only balm. Kiss a Happy Face and you'll live one more day."

"You go herb doctor. Give you some medicines you brain. No want a kiss Korean woman butt any more got a live one day."

"You don't understand."

"I understand all thing American man say Korean woman butt."

"No you don't, Ae-joo."

"You think you pretty smart guy."

"Smart enough to know some things."

"What?"

"Your butt, for example."

"Shit."

"Your butt, darling, begins right here. At the coccyx. At the tailbone. And proceeds downward and inward to here."

"Hey! Don't touch a poop place!"

"And arrives at the perineum. Which is a sort of fleshy little doormat. You can wipe your foot here and go in the back door—"

"HEY! I SAID DON'T TOUCH A POOP PLACE!"

"Or, if the fair maiden will not permit such a liberty, you can step back out and wipe your foot on the little doormat again and enter the front door like a gentleman. Like this."

"Oh!"

"And once you're inside, it's pretty dark in there. So you just feel along the wall for the light switch. Like this."

"You nice guy. Nice hand. Nice finger."

"Thank you."

"So why you no got a girlfriend?"

"I do."

"Why she no come here?"

"Because you're here. And I've got my finger inside you. Don't let's talk about her."

"She no love you?"

"So you just feel along the wall for the light switch."

"Maybe she gone a come here kill Ae-joo."

"There once was this guy who had a girlfriend whose hole was huge. Mammoth."

"Ae-joo hole too much big?"

"One night while they were making love, he thrust too hard and fell tumbling inside her."

"Your girlfriend hole too much big?"

"By the time he came to his senses, he realized he

had fallen so far in that he couldn't find his way back out again."

"Bullshit. Anybody woman no got a hole too much big like that."

"For hours he wandered around in the darkness trying to find his way out again."

"This true story? Four hours?"

"As God is my witness, Ae-joo. Finally, after he had completely lost track of even what day it was, he sat down and buried his face in his hands and wept softly."

"This guy you?"

"At the very nadir of his despair, he heard a sound off in the distance."

"This girlfriend you girlfriend?"

"There was *somebody else* inside there with him!"

"Bullshit. Now Ae-joo know bullshit."

"*Hey,* he cried. *Is there somebody else in here too?*"

"Hey! Why you put a other finger in a pussy? Ae-joo too much small. Two fingers!"

"It's part of the story, doll. Two fingers. *Sure,* said a Voice from the blackness. *I've been in here for weeks.*"

"Hurt. Don't waggle a fingers."

"*You know how to get out of here? said the man. I'm lost.*"

"This long time story."

"*Sure. No problem, said the Voice. I'll tell you what.*"

"What?"

"*I'll tell you what,* said the Voice. *You help me find my damn car keys and we'll drive out together!* HA!"

"Too long time story. You hurry finish."

"It is finished. That's the story, Ae-joo."

"Yeh? What a girlfriend say she see two guys drive out a she's pussy in a car?"

"I have no idea."

"Dumb story."

"It's a joke. Just a joke."

"Oh."

"You don't get it at all, do you?"

"Ae-joo think story girlfriend you girlfriend."

"Bull crap."

"Ae-joo think you got *goo-mung dong-suh.*"

"What the hell's that? Some kind of disease?"

"You girlfriend got a other boyfriend. You got *goo-mung dong-suh.* Same-hole brother-in-law."

"Shut up."

"Like right now. You got two fingers in Ae-joo pussy."

"And it's warm and wet in there, my sweet."

"Too much tight. No space."

"Well, spread your legs a little."

"Okay?"

"That's better."

"What you do now? You gone a climb on Ae-joo back? Make a morning time doggy jiggy-jiggy?"

"Umm."

"No put a cock in poop place. Okay?"

"Never fear."

"OH!"

"You okay, baby?"

"Uh."

"Better?"

"Why come American peoples all of time make morning time jiggy-jiggy?"

"Don't talk."

"Korean peoples think morning time jiggy-jiggy too much bad."

"Cultural differences, my love. You're Confucian. I'm a Dionysiac. We all have to make adjustments. Hitch your butt up an inch or two, could you?"

"Uh."

"That's better."

"Morning time work time. Not a jiggy-jiggy time. Sweep a floor time. Boil a rice time."

"Shhh."

"Care a babies time."

"This *is* work, baby."

"Ow!"

"Hold it right there. Now move up and down ever so slightly."

"Okay?"

"That's it. You got it."

"Oh!"

"Woooo."

"You gone a come?"

"Just hang on. Now suffer me to—"

"HEY! DON'T PUT IN A POOP PLACE! YOU PROMISE!"

"Just for a second."

"OW!"

"Oooh."

"You a Devil!"

"Wooo-ooh. Hooh!"

"You finish? You a liar. You promise. No put in a poop place. Now take out."

"Okay. Sorry."

"Hurt."

"Couldn't resist."

"You girlfriend okay put a cock in a poop place?"

"The word is 'asshole,' Ae-joo. Not 'poop place.'"

"Okay, you girlfriend okay put a cock in a asshole?"

"Don't let's talk about her."

"Who she is?"

"She's nobody."

"Can't be nobody."

"I don't have any girlfriend. Just you."

"Bullshit."

"No bullshit."

"Last night Puss 'n' Booze Club you all of time watching door. Somebody maybe come. Maybe you girlfriend come. You no buy Ae-joo whiskey coke long time."

"You're wiser than your years, baby."

"She no come, huh?"

"She no come. That's right."

"Who she is?"

"Why do you want to know?"

"Girlfriend find out you and Ae-joo jiggy-jiggy Ae-joo big trouble time."

"She doesn't care."

"She come Puss 'n' Booze Club?"

"Sometimes."

"Who she is? Got a know. Work Puss 'n' Booze Club. Maybe she come make Ae-joo big trouble time."

"Her name's Mi-ja, for Christ sake."

"Big titty Korean girl?"

"Nice talk."

"You like big titty?"

"Big tits are okay. A nice tight ass is okay too. Like yours."

"Hey! Don't put a finger in there! Ae-joo got a take some dump soon."

"Well, don't do it here in the bed."

"Big titty girl name Mi-ja. I know she. She got boyfriend. Rich England guy."

"You know him?"

"Sure. I see all of time Puss 'n' Booze Club. Big titty Mi-ja girl too. Together. Everybody know they."

"You sure?"

"Everybody know."

"Never mind. It's not important."

"You angly? You got a angly face."

"Let's change the subject."

"You love big titty Mi-ja girl, huh?"

"Are you going to can it?"

"Sorry. Don't understand."

"Forget it."

"But you love big titty Mi-ja girl. For sure."

I lift myself off the thick sleeping pad–quaintly called a *yo*–that serves as bedding over here and head into the bathroom and take a long, hard, blind piss into the toilet bowl and watch a cockroach climb the wall and disappear behind a broken tile. Mi-ja once remarked that her grandmother told her there were no cockroaches on the peninsula until the Yankees–Koreans pronounce it *yanqui,* the way Latin Americans do–steamed over for the Korean War and off-loaded the hardy little stowaways along with thousands of tons of processed American cheese in brown cardboard canisters that sat around unopened in the alleys of the cities because the half-starved, war-bitten locals couldn't stomach the bouquet of the stuff. Perhaps it is true. You never really know in Asia, where the past is forever being reinvented to bring it more in line with the tenor of the present. And vice-versa. When I finish pissing I swing my mug around in front of the mirror above the sink and start to floss out the chunky debris of last night's Pusan Blues Club beef jerky. Ae-joo comes in and sits down on the commode and commences her business, both holes, sucking in air and letting it out slowly as she purges.

"Hey," she says.

"Yes, my little heap of deep kimchi?"

"What you job?"

"*Sun-gyo-sa,*" I lie. You have to be careful. These girls talk. The Korean waitresses in the Officers Club on Base seem to know everybody. Hear everything. Smirking bitches. God help me if the Major ever got wind of this lit-

tle episode. I'd never hear the end of it. "I told you before.
I'm a missionary."

"Oh."

"Why?"

"Look at you cock."

"Oh man."

"Like you talks. Full of shits."

THE REVENGE STORY
PAY BACK

He phoned out of the blue and asked if we could get together just one more time after so many years. He had used the landline, if you can believe that. I had kept that one alive just in case—well, certainly not for *him*. Yoon—the proud son-of-a-bitch.

So we met in the old beer hall downtown just off the waterfront. He was there when I walked in, at a small table in a far corner. I couldn't believe it—the exact same table we had sat at for the very last time—six, no going on seven years back.

He appeared nervous—yet somehow relieved. Such a proud one—with his big plans back then about importing the scaffolding components he could pick up for a song from a Japanese outfit about to go bankrupt and then dump off on a local builder here for twice the price. Sure fire, he had insisted. He was just a little short at the moment—what with his wife expecting and the new apartment and all that.

The envelope appeared. Thick. Cash. He slid it across the table to me.

"It's all there," he said.

"With interest?"

"Interest!" he exclaimed wildly.

"Joking. Just kidding. Old times."

"Of course," he said, and winced. Such a proud one. It must have hurt him to wince like that.

"Still that's a lot of money."

I put my hand on top of the envelope and gave it a squeeze. I did not bother to count what was inside. Perhaps it really was all there. What was the point after so many years?

We had one beer. Then another. He talked about his wife and kids, but as if he had not seen them in a while. Such a proud man still. Not one to admit much. I took it he knew I could see the lay of it. The separation—maybe even divorce. Finally I picked up the envelope.

"You sure?" I said. "You don't have to—now."

He shrugged. Only then did I notice how shabbily he was dressed. So unlike the old Yoon. So proud.

"I pay my debts," he said. "Even if six years late."

"Going on seven," I said.

He looked at me sharply, not hurt, but a bit resentful. I had spoiled something, I suppose.

"We had been such great friends," he said.

I knew what he was driving at. He had taken me by the hand when I first arrived in his country. Showed me the ropes. The bars where you could trust the mama-sans not to pad your tab at the end of a drunken evening. The girls that—well you get the picture.

"That was a long time ago," I said.

"I'm sorry. Woefully sorry. I never should have asked for the loan. I was so sure of myself. So full of—so damned certain. I should have known those damned Japanese would pull a fast one and stiff me."

His pride had deflated. It was gone. He looked like one of those flat fish laid out in so many rows in a market stall. Finally. After so many years of silence and evasion. Of changing his phone numbers. His home addresses, such as they were. His "new apartment"—if there ever really had been one. I had long ago given up on tracking him down.

"Well," I said. "Maybe it was my fault. Maybe I should have known better."

"No," he said. "Don't blame yourself."

"Well, I had been warned."

He stared back with a sort of stupid incredulity—and blinked.

"Pardon me?"

"Well, people had warned me. About loaning you—"

"What!" he shot back in anger. Pride and anger. "What! WHO?"

"Your friends back then. You know."

"WHO?" he demanded. He was furious. "It can't be true! Tell me who!"

"Just—you know . . *people*."

"People? People! I never—nobody—how could–"

He was trembling all over. For a moment I thought he might actually seize me by the throat. But his thoughts were jumping. I believe his mind was running down lists of old friends. Classmates in the night school where I had taught them all Business English, I was sure. Which of them might have considered him a bad risk—a chancer, big talker, wheeler-dealer extraordinaire.

"Nobody," I said. "Forget it."

He was looking down into his lap now and shaking his head from side to side and mumbling to himself.

"Who would say such a thing about me? Mr. Yang? Mrs. Choi? That ignoramus Mr. Pak? No, not even him. Not Mr. Moon. No. Never. Miss Kim she always–"

So I was glad to ease myself away from the table and make my way to the door—with the envelope secure in my jacket pocket now. It had been a cruel lie. I had thought about it for years. Planned it. Practically recited it. Wondered if I would ever really get the chance. Still I was shocked—appalled almost—at how nimbly it had rolled off my tongue.

A month later I ran into Mr. Moon in the lobby of the Cineplex. It had been years. A nice coincidence. Fittingly they were screening Old Classics that week. I had not seen *Gaslight* since film class back in my college days—in another country, on another continent. And here I was on the arm of a woman from another culture. Another world even. She of the landline kept open for. Things were looking up.

"Have you seen Mr. Yoon recently by any chance?" he asked. "You must remember him and his swagger and little schemes, of course. Well, he's running around and looking up all of his old classmates from night school. And driving us all crazy. Imploring everyone if we think he's honest—a straight-shooter, or some such foolishness. We think maybe there's something wrong with the man. Really wacko, maybe. Possibly a nut case, we're afraid. Do you think perhaps you could have a word with the guy? Talk to him. Reason with him. You know, he always looked up to you. We always used to joke that you were the only one of our professors he ever truly admired."

THE SHAGGY DOG STORY
AT PLAY IN THE YEAR OF THE DOG

"**N**O!" I howl. "I CAN'T!"

Mr. Choi glowers down at the small oblong plate on which lies the pathetic fountain-pen-size tube of boiled flesh. Gentle Mr. Ku sits stiffly upright, nervously fingering his stainless steel chopsticks with the ginseng root patterns on the handle-ends, fidgety fearful that he has been made an accomplice in some terrible breach of etiquette—at the expense of an honorable foreigner, no less. Impish Mr. Kim, who has been rubbing his palms together with gleeful anticipation, knocks back a glass of clear, potent *soju*. Once a month the four of us dine out together, trading ribald jokes, ribbing each other about our respective governments' blunders and inexhaustible capacities for mismanagement, consoling one and all on our own respective failures to "get ahead," rambling on in our cups about sex and money and power and corruption—that which concerns all men at all times in all lands. The principal at the high school where Mr. Kim's brother-in-law teaches was recently arrested for taking hundreds of thousands of dollars in bribes from parents who wanted their kids' grade transcripts doctored. The President-for-Life at a local university was dethroned not so long ago by mobs of student demonstrators for permitting the matriculation of students who had failed the entrance exam but had succeeded in life by having rich, well-connected fathers and steel-willed mothers of vise-like tenacity who would not see their children's lives flushed down the tubes just because the pampered, indolent brats had neither brains, nor ambition, nor talent. Nobody quite understood why this university president bothered to take these bribes—he was already one of the wealthiest men in the province. Perhaps it was only because, as one Korean Sage-cum-Wag puts it, "For a Korean with a desk and a nameplate of inlaid mother-of-pearl, going a month without a bribe is like going five hundred years without a woman."

But tonight was to have been a special night. The focus was to have been on the meal itself, and not on peripheral concerns like our indignation and utter amazement at what blatant sleaziness our fellow professionals have proved themselves capable of. My three Korean high school English teachers had been on me for months now to overcome my deepest personal inhibitions and narrow cultural prejudices and try *gaegogi*—boiled dog meat. And, I decide, I have acquitted myself well this evening, munching through a respectable portion of slices of abdominal wall of pooch, a large platter of dark, tender morsels of haunch of pooch, and a helping of sweet and succulent, melt-in-your-mouth neck of pooch. I couldn't quite manage to handle my share of the four steaming paws we had been served up, soft budlike footpads intact—staring at them in bafflement and gingerly turning one over and then glancing beseechingly at each of my hosts. When the "auntie" set them down on the low table where the four of us sat cross-legged, I at first mistook them for a version of braised pussy willow, so difficult it is for the mind to recognize on a plate what it has a thousand times registered in living rooms and back yards: *Shake hands, Abelard. Now roll over. Now beg. Don't you have the cutest little footsies. Kiss.*

And then finally on to the evening's coup de coeur—er, cur:

"I'm sorry, Mr. Kim. I just CAN'T!"

Mr. Choi and Mr. Ku stare at each other and then down at the little weenie that has been cut for us into four equal measures, uncertain whether it would be polite to partake. This final delectable of the meal would be getting cold. It has always been my friends' custom to offer me the first, choicest morsel of anything set before us. I am a foreigner and in middle-middle age—that laughable euphemism whose threshold is crossed with only the deepest misgivings—nearly a decade their senior to boot. And a college professor, or at least a reasonable simulacrum thereof. A man of profound learning and broad experience. A man who washed down a bull's testicle tapa with a pitcher of tinto in the shadow of the bullring in Jerez on that other *peninsula de tristeza*. Hemingwayesque. Almost a hero in the eyes of my nephews, who applauded the snapshot I sent home to my sister of yours truly running the bulls down main street in Arcos de la Frontera. But this little finger of canine flesh, licked a thousand times under summer suns by its former owner—

"Professor Proctor," Mr. Kim coaxes. "Couldn't you just close your eyes? I'll slip it right in your mouth."

"He's chicken," Mr. Choi grumbles.

"I'm sorry," I whine. "I just don't think I can. You never told me we'd be eating the dog's *jaji*!"

Which is true. Mr. Kim had extracted the dogmeat promise from me that afternoon over the phone. But he never mentioned *jaji*. Like a lover wheedling a kiss out of his virginal sweetheart, Mr. Kim had insisted that I didn't know what I was missing. *It not only tastes good. Gaegogi is good for you too. You've been in Korea long enough. It's time!* This was only too true too. I had been making jokes in poems and stories about Koreans and dog meat for long enough, maintaining the practice was symptomatic of something darker and more sinister lurking just behind the culture's sunny smile—packed between its molars, in fact. But, in all fairness, did I know whereof I spoke regarding pooch and Culture and the culinary arts? *And Mr. Ku hasn't been feeling up to par lately. He needs it for his health. His stamina.* Which, of course, had always been my point. That Korean men eat dog to give their sex lives a boost and a boast—to produce rock-hard erections that must last well into the matutinal ministrations of amor. A stiff prick is just plain good health. "Never loan money to a man who wakes up in the morning without a hard-on," runs a venerable Sino-Korean proverb, meaning, obviously, Be careful the fucker doesn't croak before he has the chance to pay you back. And I'm sure Mr. Ku's wife would appreciate it too. They're still hoping for that male offspring. And they're not getting any younger. That the birth of a bouncing baby boy might hinge on a dog hanging by its neck from a hook on the ceiling of a butcher shop and slowly choking to death because the adrenaline invoked by the suffering is thought to tenderize the meat is, of course, my point even more poignantly. *And this is The Year of the Dog! And you were a Dog Year baby! You said so! Professor Proctor, please!*

Clearly it is now or never. The success or failure of the evening rests in my carnivorous claws. Gruff, rock-jawed Mr. Choi sits in gloom as the boiled dog's boiled *jaji* cools down to the ambient temperature. Mild, self-effacing Mr. Ku looks on with pained resignation. Convivial Mr. Kim leans forward and beams boyishly in my face. He has already taken pains to make his point that the "auntie"—who is in fact the owner of the establishment—graces only the most "esteemed" clients with this special "cut." I make an effort to recall that eminently versatile syllogism a Real Man is trained to employ in difficult circumstances: *In this situation everybody always has a good time. I am in this situation. Therefore I am having a good time.* With trembling chopsticks I lift my quarter of dog *jaji* and deposit it on my tongue. Chew and chew and finally gulp and swallow, stifling the gag reflex with that same power of sheer will a man might beseech a novice fellatrix to summon in the throes of an analogous consummation. Wash down whatever debris remains with a toss of sweet, viscous *soju*. The welkin does not open up. Nor does a bolt of lightning come bursting through the window of the restaurant to split me in half like a forlorn, solitary oak in a thunderstorm. No Marlow out of Conrad comes chugging slowly downriver to carry my final whispers back to genteel drawingroom civilization. Dog pizzle, it is clear, when properly prepared, is—well, edible. And yes, since you're dying to ask, there indeed is a bone in it. The lucky stiffs.

*

At a beer house far enough off the beaten track to be reasonably priced—a *dan-gol jip* or "regular haunt" of Mr. Kim's and our *ee-cha* or "second stop" for the evening—a waitress in a miniskirt and about a quart of cheap domestic perfume sets down a bilingual menu before us. Mr. Choi, eager to show off his English in front of the young and aromatic sexpot, orders four bottles of OB beer and something called "Dried Slices of Dish," which turns out to be regular old *marun anju*, a mixed plate of dried anchovies, tissue-thin squares of dried seaweed, peanuts and tiny strips of dried cuttlefish. As a fan of tales of the grotesque I feel obliged to suggest the "Dried Poe"—I wonder how long the poor bastard had been walled up before adjudged desiccated enough to serve as provender—but Mr. Ku waves me off and indicates that what we really need to balance (this is *yin-yang* country, after all, or more properly *um-yang*, as Koreans style it) the *marun anju* is the risible "Fruited Prate" which, in due turn, manifests itself as a simple platter of sliced apples and bananas and segments of mandarin orange. In Korea it is considered barbaric and "unreasonable to your health" to drink without a snack at your fingertips—even if you have just polished off a sizeable portion of Man's Best Friend, pecker, neck, haunch and paw.

"I've got good news for you, Professor Proctor," Mr. Kim announces as he pours me a glass of beer from one of the oversize bottles of OB. In Korea it is regarded as the epitome of anti-social audaciousness to pour your own. Koreans may be among the world's most prodigious boozers, but every form of excess here is governed by principles of etiquette ignored only at the risk of jeopardizing the eternal serenity of one's dead Ancestors. A man reckless enough to be found drinking alone in a bar might as well be declaring to all the world that he doesn't have any family or friends—and doesn't give a shit, either.

"Shoot."

"You mentioned on the phone that you wanted to start putting away some money."

"I suspect it's about time."

"Well, there's a terrific savings plan at the Korea Finance Bank. For teachers only. Twelve percent a year."

"Twelve percent? You think I'm eligible?"

"Why not? You're a teacher—just like us."

"Yeh, but I'm a foreigner too. And you know what that means."

"Here," he says, removing a slip of memo paper from his pocket. "I wrote down the name of the savings plan for you in Korean. Just show it to the people at the downtown branch. No problem. Don't worry. You're one of us!"

I pocket the note, sit back, and hoist my glass of beer. Mr. Choi, an exuberant master-of-ceremonies now that he has half a bottle of *soju* and a goodly portion of pooch under his belt, proposes a toast and we all drink to something I don't quite catch. Something about "your ancestor's dog's corpse." Mr. Kim senses my confusion and offers to translate: "May wild dogs rummage your grandmother's bones."

"That's not a toast," I cry. "That's a curse."

"Yes," Mr. Choi laughs. "But it's a Family Curse! Ha! My father used to shout it when he drank with his friends in the old days. Then the others would join in and recite their own favorite curses. I learned a lot from them."

I allow that it's a heck of a good curse and Mr. Choi scribbles it down for me in Korean on another piece of memo paper. I pocket this note too, with the notion of committing it to memory when I have a clearer head, certain that I will have the opportunity to use it sooner or later—no doubt the next time a taxi driver refuses to stop for my Caucasoid Mug in front of my school or some bargirl tries to hit me up for a 10,000 *won* whiskey coke. Mr. Ku asks me the most effective curse in English and I tell him my old stand-by. He begs me to write it down for him (it's the one about *You and the horse you rode in on*) and soon curses and slips of white memo paper are flying so fast and thick we probably look like four drunken louts simultaneously stricken with a wacky strain of Gilles de la Tourrette's Syndrome in the middle of an arctic blizzard. My three friends have spent much of their waking professional lives studying and teaching textbook English, but they often fess up to an uneasiness about certain gaps in their knowledge. They are innocent of the "juicier" recesses of my native tongue and sometimes feel like bewildered outsiders (a condition of the spirit I know only too well) when they view Hollywood films laced with racy slang and raunchy obscenities. In the Korean subtitles to American movies, "asshole," "cocksucker" and "motherfucker" all come out as the more blandly comprehensive *gaejashik*, "offspring of a cur." There is, really, no appropriate lexicon for my friends save for a native speaker with a few too many beers in him. They need me—and if world politics are any guide—this may be the only real foundation for international friendship.

"What's a 'cunt head'?" growls Mr. Choi. "I cannot imagine this. Or a 'dick head'? I cannot imagine this either."

"They're just other words for 'asshole,' I suppose. Like 'shit for brains' or 'dog breath' or 'butt face'."

"Well, why do you Americans need so many words for 'asshole'?"

Which is a hell of a good question. Signifiers and Things Signified. Signs and Wonders. But it is late in the evening—not the hour to mutate from a beer-swilling dogeater into a Theory-spewing frogeater. "I guess it just goes," I say, "with the territory."

*

Mr. Choi and Mr. Ku live near each other on the other side of town and, after conferring secretively with Mr. Kim on some arcane matter that involves the exchange of fistfuls of banknotes, choose to share a taxi home. The cab gets only a dozen yards down the street when Mr. Ku springs out and dashes back into the beer house. He emerges minutes later with the foil packet of leftover *gaegogi* that his wife had entreated him to bring home. She wants that little *puer* heir as much as he does. Mr. Ku waves as the taxi lurches off again. Mr. Kim and I wave back. The gentle English teacher hadn't forgotten about his "doggy bag"—which, I have the opportunity to observe, is no mere figure of speech over here. I stand on the street corner ready to flag down the next cab while Mr. Kim circles around me in an eccentric orbit, eyeing me up and down appraisingly. Above us a streetlamp buzzes and flickers. It is a weeknight and downtown has long since turned in.

"How do you feel?" Mr. Kim asks.

"Fine. A little bushed, I guess."

"You didn't eat much of the *gaegogi*."

"I had my share, I think. Thank you."

"You look like you could do with a haircut."

"Don't be silly," I snap. "I had one just last week."

"A trim then," he says flatly. "I know a place nearby."

"Mr. Kim, it's almost midnight. There aren't any barbershops open now. Even if I wanted a haircut."

"This one is special."

Mr. Kim hooks my arm and ushers me across the street. A taxi without a fare slows to a crawl and I motion for it to pull over but Mr. Kim tugs on my coatsleeve insistently and the cab draws off. We walk down a narrow sidestreet of darkened, closed shops that opens on a broad thoroughfare. Beside the entrance of a new office building a carpeted flight of steps leads down to a subterranean glass door curtained on the inside.

"That barber pole is not lit up, Mr. Kim. It isn't revolving. This place is closed."

"The police," he says conspiratorially. "You've read about the crackdown."

As indeed everyone has. Korea has been polishing up its public image ever since its capital won the venue for the '88 Olympics. This involves, naturally enough, the eradication of all appearances of public vice—particularly lewd services for hire. But Mr. Kim has never seemed the type to frequent such places. He is happily married, or so he says. I met his wife once and liked her. No beauty, she has that grace that comes when a woman is sincerely content with her husband. Teachers are underpaid in Korea, but thanks to Confucius and Mencius and all that crowd their social status is high. Traffic cops will let you off with a warning if you flash your school ID card. You are a *son-saeng-nim*. *Son-saeng* means "teacher." *Nim* is a special tag used with certain forms of address and means "honorable." (*Nom*, interestingly, is its precise opposite. But I won't go into that. Suffice to say, you watch your vowels over here.)

Mr. Kim pushes open the glass door and I follow him into a small, low-ceilinged waiting room lined on three sides with sturdy, well-worn sofas. There is a hint of mildew and a clammy closeness in the air; we are indeed underground. A young woman in heavy makeup and a sort of beautician's uniform sits on one of the sofas engrossed in a dubbed Hollywood movie on a tiny portable TV. Gregory Peck is taking lip from a woman at a lavish party. Then the woman is crying and people around them are beginning to notice. He appears about to visit the face of the teary-eyed beauty with the back of his hand when the young woman notices us standing inside the door and jumps off her sofa and bends down to remove my shoes. She sets down a pair of plastic shower sandals and guides my feet into them.

"I'll wait here," Mr. Kim says solemnly. "I'm a married man. I get twinges of consciousness. You're a bachelor. You don't get enough relief. Besides, I haven't seen this movie before. I like William Holden."

"That's Gregory Peck," I say. "That's not William Holden."

"Of course," Mr. Kim stares hard at the television screen and squints.

In a cubicle barely spacious enough for jumpingjacks the young woman in the beautician's uniform settles me in a barber chair, tucks my collar inside my shirt, and checks the length of my fingernails, all the while discretely averting her eyes. From underneath all that makeup nothing specific, nothing individual shines through, save that she has a widow's peak and a dimpled chin. Such Asian women, a likeable but thoroughly unreliable ex-Peace Corps Volunteer once titillated me, sport no foliage on their fleshy little venereal escarpments. But clothed she might be any porcelain doll in a row of identical porcelain dolls in a toy shop window, passive, wide-eyed, inert yet hypnotically alert.

A barber in a starched white tunic enters and wordlessly goes about the business of giving me a trim. The straight razor is dull and rasps at my nape, and I think about weasels ripping my flesh and the late Frank Zappa and middle age and inoperable cancer of the prostate. The barber doesn't so much finish the job as seem to lose interest and give up. He packs up his tools in a drawer beneath the large mirror in front of the barber chair and sort of melts away. I don't know how else to describe it—he is there in the mirror one moment and then he is smaller and then he is gone. Dimpled Chin returns—perhaps she ducked out to catch part of the Gregory Peck flick with Mr. Kim—and pulls a lever of some sort underneath the chair and suddenly the back of the chair collapses and I am staring up at the ceiling, my legs stuck straight out and supported by a part of the chair that has risen magically up out of nowhere. A neat gadget, I decide. Dimpled Chin places a small towel over my eyes—some small concession to female modesty, no doubt—but I can see fairly well out the lower edge, as in cheating at Pin-the-Tail-on-the-Donkey. Then the overhead light goes out and a red lamp above the mirror comes on. Apparently there are hidden levers and toggles all over the place, like a state-of-the-art torture chamber. She sits down beside me on a low stool and massages my arm, popping my fingers on one end and squeezing my pectorals on the other. Occasionally her hand drifts over my belly and brushes lightly across my lap, each time tarrying there a little longer, applying just the slightest bit more pressure. It is all very coy but my chest tightens just the same and my breathing begins to labor. With cool precision she unzips my fly and unbuckles my belt, guiding me to arch my back just enough for her to slide my slacks and undershorts down to mid-thigh. There are stirrings. The sluggish juices have begun to roil.

By methodically squinching and unsquinching my face I am able to dislodge the towel enough to clap eye fully on my manly part. That poor, abused appendage is engorging admirably. Perhaps it is the angle of perspective or a trick of the red glow in the background, but the thing looks huge, alien, and eerily majestic, like an inscrutable dolmen thrust up on the horizon at the scarlet dawn of time. (Rosy pose, empurpled prose.) No better hung than the next White Dude, I have to allow that maybe there is something to this dog-meat aphrodisiac business after all. And then my cock vanishes and the silhouette of her head appears in its place, bobbing up and down, up and down, her lips doing all the heavy work, her teeth carefully tucked away in the soft, pliant flesh inside her mouth. I close my eyes and try hard not to think of epileptic seizures or the set of barber's tools packed in the drawer just an arm's length away in the dark. That morning's editorial in the paper complained that not only had Lorena Bobbit been found innocent by reason of temporary insanity, she has been released from the loony bin with a clean bill of mental health as well. In Thailand, the editorial went on, wronged, indignant wives refer jocularly to the act of castrating one's husband as "throwing him to the ducks." More poetically, in the Philippines, where surgeons are adept at reattaching severed organs, one feminist critic has suggested tying the bloody thing to a helium-filled balloon and releasing it to the sodden, moon-drenched Manila night sky.

*

Mr. Kim is watching the credits of the Gregory Peck movie when I step back into the waiting room, struggling to control the fool smirk of the blissfully undone torturing my lips. Dimpled Chin bows deeply to the two of us as I lift my feet out of the plastic sandals and settle them into the familiarity of my loafers. Mr. Kim slips her a small pad of banknotes and she bows again. She says something in dialect that I do not catch and Mr. Kim laughs and agrees with her. He tells her I am an important professor from a foreign country and her hand covers her mouth in a manner that suggests reverential awe—or panicked confusion, sometimes it is hard to tell which. She bows hurriedly a third time and backs away and disappears through the narrow archway that leads to the cluster of hidden cubicles, shielding her face as from, I muse, the Brightness and Glory of My Countenance. After all, I am still grinning like a loon.

"Mr. Choi and Mr. Ku and I were worried about you," Mr. Kim remarks as he levers me into a taxi out on the street again. "You're a bachelor. You never talk about a girlfriend."

"You guys all chipped in, didn't you?"

Mr. Kim smiles paternally. The taxi driver drums his fingers on the dashboard.

"We are all thankful for what you have done for us."

Toward dawn I awaken in my bed, bolt upright and shivering, my torso and arms rigid in a straitjacket of cold sweat. I have been tossing a stick in a green meadow and a prancing, eager mixed-breed—it is my Natasha whom I had had to let a vet put down so many years back—is retrieving it for me. Each time she brings it back I pat her on the head and let her lick my face and nuzzle me down below. On the last throw she returns with a limp human penis clutched gingerly in her jaws. I look down between my legs but there is nothing there, only a bloody round hole the size of a half dollar. Natasha ducks and feints playfully and dashes away with her prize in her mouth as I stand fast, frozen, unable to pursue, a shock of her tawny hair in my clenched fist.

*

I slip the piece of memo paper out of my wallet and present it to the pretty young teller with bangs and a button nose at the downtown branch of the Korea Finance Bank. She unfolds it, scans the message and pauses, mumming her lips as in silent prayer. Then she gapes up at me, her bright, innocent eyes wide with incomprehension and her lips slightly parted, as if one of us has suddenly been revealed a couple of beads short in the old abacus.

"*Son-saeng imnida*," I mince with an ingratiating, rehearsed smile. "I'm a teacher. Special account. Twelve percent. For teachers only."

Bangs and Button Nose eases herself nervously off of her tiny stool behind the counter and hurries the note to a desk along the back wall of the bank where a serious man in a salaryman's blue suit is flipping mechanically through a stack of cashier's checks. They confer, whispering behind cupped hands and glancing over at me from time to time. Bangs and Button Nose's expression has changed from bewildered confusion to pallid, abject terror. Salaryman turns the note around and around, as if reading it upside-down or backwards might yield up the information he seeks. A security guard eyes me with suspicion—it is, of course, not all that wise to pass a handwritten note to a bank teller, regardless of the culture you find yourself in. I stare impatiently at the pair, summoning an air of indignation at the delay. No doubt I will be asked to produce a ream of documents to prove I am a teacher and eligible for the savings plan. When at long last Salaryman rises from behind his desk and approaches the counter, he clears his throat and bows slightly. Tiny pearls of sweat glisten on his forehead just below the hairline.

"Sir," he says in crisp, polite English. "Miss Gong is new to her position at our bank. This is her second week only. Clearly it would be better if I spoke with you."

"I understand completely," I say, pitying poor Bangs and Button Nose, who is now a terror-stricken silhouette against the blank wall. Her pose reminds me of a postcard someone once sent me from Pompeii. She has probably never met a foreigner face to face before. Whatever English she might have been able to muster in a high school classroom a year before has failed her in the breach. The challenge of a simple conversation in a foreign tongue is an impossible burden for such kids, like being asked to play ping-pong with a bowling ball.

"On the other hand," Salaryman continues, creasing and smoothing out the note in his hands, "clearly there has been some mistake. This—"

Some mistake. I know that song and dance. I hear it from Immigration Officials every year when I try to renew my residence card. I heard it from the Ministry of Education when they demanded copies of my dusty university diplomas if they were to approve me to teach here in The Land of the 10,000 Bureaucratic Rudenesses. I heard it from the City Courthouse when I went to apply for the form I would need to apply for the documents necessary to apply for a marriage license, documents finally procured the day before I got dumped. Now it is the banks' turn.

"I'm not eligible for the account? Because I'm a foreigner? Fine," I snap sarcastically, not bothering for an answer. "Thanks." I snatch the note out of his hands, thrust it into my jacket pocket, spin around on my heels and storm out of the building.

Outside I look up and down the street for a taxi stand.

Behind the glass doors of the bank Salaryman is speaking at length with a nodding security guard. Traffic whizzes by a few feet from my nose, swirling the air and sending scraps of paper in dizzying spirals high above the cracked, uneven sidewalk. A sewer opening reeks at my feet. And suddenly a queer sensation sweeps over me. That twinge of paralysis you feel when you realize you can't remember for sure whether or not you unplugged the coffee pot before you left home in the morning. I fish the note out of my pocket and uncrumple it and translate the scribbled Korean with gut-wrenching humiliation and a blinding rush of profound sympathy for poor Miss Bangs and Button Nose: *May wild dogs rummage your grand—*

THE MONOLOGUE FLASH STORY
STEAM IRONS OF DESIRE

I.

We all have our tribulations–those of us who live far from our native lands. We all want to square what we feel is just and fair with the human nature on display around us. Mostly, though, we just want to *understand*. For months now, for instance, I've been trying to figure out what Koreans do to their steam irons on the weekends. I don't know what they do, but I believe they must grievously mistreat their steam irons on the weekends. The situation is this: My phone number is 8-6-1-1. The phone number of the Philips people–the Dutch company that markets quality steam irons here in Korea–is 8-6-6-1. (I won't burden you with my three-digit prefix. And I get my share of phantom rings and crank prank calls these days as it is.) Every Monday morning I receive at least one wrong number phone call. It's always somebody who wants to talk to Philips. Or *Pee-leeps*, if you like. It's always a guy with a hoarse hungover wheeze or else a housewife-sounding lady in a state of near panic who wants me to connect them to the Steam Iron Repair Department. This is as much as I care to get out of them. I tell them I'm a foreigner–*Way-kook saram imnida*–and then they hang up. Sometimes they call right back again with the same routine and sometimes it takes them just the one shot to figure out who I'm not. I'm not the Philips Steam Iron Repair Department. Never was. No connection with them at all. Of course nothing of this speaks to my original perplexity, which is what Koreans do to their steam irons on the weekends. Quite frankly I'm baffled. I know this is another culture and I'm not supposed to question their ways. Their ways are just as beautiful as my own–only different. But they are doing something to their steam irons on the weekends that is probably not nice. Maybe I should call up the UN. Maybe they could refer me to some do-gooder NGO that handles missions like this. Or maybe I should just shut up and mind my own business. It's just that on Monday mornings I like to start the week right. I like to get off on the right foot, so to speak, on the first morning of the new week. Especially after the things I do and don't do on the long, lonely weekends here in Korea. And I don't even own a steam iron here in Korea. I don't have one, which upon reflection may lie at the root of all my bewilderment.

II.

So I go out and buy myself a Philips steam iron. A nice one. Top of the line, in fact. A Philips Propavore Aurora Mistral 4000 with a Karezza™ soleplate, nine heat settings, continuous steam output of up to 40g/min as well as a 90g Shot o' Steam™. I even buy an ironing board to set this baby on. One of those Asian-style ironing boards that sits just a few inches off the floor. One of those ironing boards that look like they're designed for legless amputees or other unfortunates. The weekend rolls around and I wait to see what's going to happen. Friday night. Nothing. All day Saturday and then Saturday night. Nothing and again nothing. Sunday morning and then Sunday afternoon. Ditto. Nada. So it's Sunday night. My new Philips Propavore Aurora Mistral 4000 sits there on the ironing board with its four stubby legs like some sort of prehistoric earth-hugging creature mounted on its mother's back. Good, I decide. At least something's happening. In my imagination, anyway. Of course Sunday nights are lonely times for bachelors like me. All the pent up frustration of a thousand misspent weekends begins to seethe. The sense of wasted life. The intimations of a profound and nameless disconnectedness and despair. I plug the steam iron into the wall socket and crank it up to Heat Setting Nine because I am fed up with feeling so damn lonely on

Sunday nights. I want what people call an "objective cor-relative." Some damn object out there in the world that feels what I feel. That knows and shares my solitude and isolation. The steam iron starts to get hot. Hotter. Cocked back on its haunch now, it's even heating up the room. I mean it's really cooking. I wet the tip of my finger with a film of saliva and touch the steam iron's smooth underbelly. YOWCH! That's HOT! So hot and yet so smooth too. I stroke the steam iron's smooth underbelly again, this time without the protective film of saliva. It's HOT as HELL. I mean it's really HOT. With a blistered fingertip I press the Red Button on the handle of the steam iron and mar-vel–*SSSSSST!*–at the sheer primal force and energy of its 90g Shot o' Steam™. But it's not enough. It's just nowhere near enough. I want to touch the damn thing in a way no steam iron has ever been touched before. I want the smooth underbelly of the damn thing tonight and I don't care what happens to either of us. Steam irons of course are not designed for this sort of relationship. This sort of household *ménage*. They are designed for ironing clothes. And not even all kinds of clothes. Certainly not for the kind of thing I have in mind. Not for the kind of thing that seems to me, now, suddenly, inevitable. I unplug my Philips Propavore Aurora Mistral 4000 and let her cool down, let her slip deep into the untroubled dreamless sleep of unplugged home appliances. Helpless now, she rides there on the back of her ironing board mother like some forlorn species of fabulous sleeping snail beast that time forgot. I reach out and pluck her off, cradle her iron shell in my aching arms, and hiss into her smooth soleplate my basest secrets, my crudest yearnings, my purest and most unspeakable human animal needs.

III.

The next morning–Monday morning—I call up Philips and ask for the Steam Iron Repair Department. I talk to a sweet young thing who I imagine is sitting primly at a desk in a cluttered office. Perhaps she is sitting behind a window that looks out on the shop floor. Perhaps she is wearing a name tag that identifies her as "Miss Kim." In fractured Korean I try to tell her what happened. What I need. She listens attentively, the soul of patience and empathy. She understands exactly what happened. How these things happen. What a client needs. She understands exactly what is wrong. I don't have to explain. That, she assures me intimately, is why she is there.

PART TWO:
MEMOIR INTROMISSION

STAKEOUTS & STINGS:
FOUR BACKFLUNG GEEZER GLANCES

DUKE, THE DUCHESSES
AND DURHAM BURNING

It was just past 7 PM and I was out of Marlboros. The Raleigh tv station reported the curfew had been lifted in the capital, in Charlotte, Winston-Salem, Wilmington, etc., now that the riots were officially over. I had been indoors alone all day in my cramped two-room off campus digs writing a paper on John Webster's *The White Devil* for Prof. Blackburn and paid no attention to the world darkening outside. Prof. Blackburn's brooding face and booming, unsettling laugh guaranteed you did not want to plead for an extension on your assignment. Mine was due the next day and I still had a half dozen pages to go. I calculated I would be up to well past midnight and I needed my smokes.

I suppose I had gotten within maybe twenty or thirty yards of the 7-11 parking lot before I realized my car was surrounded by National Guardsmen. Funny how I had not noticed the streets were empty and the lights in the windows of the 7-11 were not on. I did not even notice the

Guardsmen approach. They were just there on stakeout in the dark and I was surrounded by them.

Nice fucking move, Ass Brain, I am sure I thought in the back seat of the squad car with a National Guardsman on either side of me. Maybe I was frisked, I don't remember. No doubt I was. But no handcuffs. I was white. And I am sure they believed me when I told them I had just ducked out for a pack of cigarettes. Only later that evening would we entertain the jailhouse rumor that a particularly reviled local furniture store had been put to the torch the night before and that was why the curfew had not been lifted in Durham.

We all smoked in those days. Smoked in class, even. The school provided classrooms with little cardboard and foil ashtrays scattered here and there on the desk chairs we sat in. The hot black roots peroxide blonde—yep, we called them that back then—who sat next to me in Prof. Blackburn's class smoked too, never finishing a cigarette before stubbing it out and lighting another. She had published a story in the school magazine about a Black woman who cannibalizes a white man in an elevator. I don't remember the details, of course, but I thought it very daring and sophisticated. Certainly she would be a Real Writer someday. She was slim and angular and sexy with long, nervous, tapered fingers and a plash of freckles across her cheeks. The freckles did not belong in this suite somehow. But this just made her the more exotic and desirable. They did not detract from the fact that she had Class. It was all I could do not to steal a glance at her every chance I got. It was all I could do to force myself to stare straight ahead at Prof. Blackburn's baleful, batrachian countenance.

Before I was locked up for the night the officer behind the desk informed me I would be given the opportunity to post bond in the morning. Fortunately I had the five or ten bucks on me, whatever it was, that served as a sort of down payment. There would be a bail-bondsman already there at a little table and maybe we would have to wait in line. There were some other stragglers there who had been caught off campus ducking behind hedges and shrubs on their furtive, circuitous paths back to their dorms after dark—and a handful of clueless townies as well. It did not sink in at first that we were all white. All I really cared about was that I would be released in the morning when the curfew expired at 6 AM.

The jail inside the courthouse was spacious enough. The individual cells had been swung open and you could wander listlessly from one to the other or just sit on one of the wooden benches in the main area behind the big wall of bars. It was all quite casual. Clearly we curfew breakers were not deemed dangerous–either to ourselves or others.

On a wall in one of the cells some wag had scrawled a few lines from *The Ballad of Reading Gaol*. I had not read the poem at the time and only knew *The Picture of Dorian Gray* from the movies. If I had heard Oscar Wilde was gay I probably would have assumed it was because he was an Artist–a Lonely and Sensitive Genius. After I had settled in on a wooden bench and established a modicum of personal jail space one of the guards appeared and announced he would procure us cigarettes for two bits a pack. Yep, you read that right. This was Durham, North Carolina. They might deprive you of your freedom for a night but they would never dream of depriving you of a smoke. I finally got my Marlboros.

I did not know it at the time that Prof. Blackburn was a legend in his own right–that he had mentored the likes of William Styron and Anne Tyler. *The Confessions of Nat Turner* had been published the year before but I had not read it yet. I was still struggling with *Humphrey Clinker* and *Portrait of a Lady*. In class I never volunteered a peep, surrounded as I was with some of the brightest girls American university life had to offer. But you could not hide in a horseshoe seating arrangement and I remember being spectacularly slow-witted when called upon to comment on a disquietingly macabre passage in *The Duchess of Mal-fi: The spring in his face is nothing but the engendering of toads.* Fortunately I was too thick with the callowness of youth to sense it might be some sort of a dare: Prof. Blackburn was himself pushing seventy and the decades had not been kind. (I understand, Sir, now, Sir.) To be fair, the coeds in the class–and it was all girls, save myself and one other lost soul of a guy—were almost as intimidated as I was. They were smooth in their responses to his questions but stammered breathlessly when tasked to read a sonnet aloud. One afternoon toward the end of the hour Prof. Blackburn dropped a quotation on us: "My reputation! I've lost my reputation! I've lost the immortal part of me!" He scoured the horseshoe for hands. None rose. "*Othello!*" I ejaculated proudly, my arm in the air. "Lieutenant Cassio." Had I known his serial number I probably would have given that too. I had seen the Olivier version a few months earlier and had been moved by the good officer's plight. It was the finest moment of my career in college. The young and brilliant lovelies in the class twisted in their desk chair seats and yawned. The hour was up.

At first the jailhouse chatter was idle and inconsequential. None of us was there as a matter of Conscience. Dr. King had been shot a few days before and we students held a Silent Vigil the next day on the Main Quad in front of the Chapel with its statue of Robert E. Lee inside. No tear gas, though. That would have to wait another year. But we were in the tank because we were dumb fucks who got caught out on the street after dark. Nevertheless we did finally manage to piece together why maybe the curfew had not been lifted in Durham. That last furniture store that burned down was a focal point of resentment, so the story went, among the Black population of the town. If you know anything about installment plans and the Repo Man you can probably guess why. No doubt the local KKK knew this too. Even today historians debate whether or not Hitler had the Reichstag burned down. Whether it was a False Flag operation or not. And only the year before a couple of classmates of mine had tried to get a peek at a Klan rally and gotten their eyes blackened and their noses bloodied in the parking lot for their trouble. They came back to campus looking like bushwhacked pandas.

Toward dawn after we had mostly dozed off on the wooden benches on our floor of the city jail, the singing began. I don't remember what song it was. I like to think it was We Shall Overcome but I can't swear to it. The Blacks who had been picked up that night were behind bars in their own cell block on the floor below us. Their voices lifted in proud and defiant unison and those of us who were still awake stared at each other in stunned silence and wonder and a sudden and inexplicable shiver, or was it perhaps a shudder, of envy and shame.

The afternoon JS walked out of prison after two years and a month on the inside his parents were waiting in the station wagon with Karen. From the parking lot they all drove across the river to the Justice of the Peace on the Ohio side. This was the big part of the deal. A married JS could go back to college on his parents' dime and pick up his life where it had broken off.

JS had met Karen on work release but this was all I knew from his letters. The juicy details had been left between the lines in order the pass the censor's scrutiny. The prison psychologist was a careful man and had even made a few astute comments on the poems I was sending JS at the time. Scatological was the word he used, I think, and I appreciated that. I was as much in love with language in those days as an incarcerated JS was in love with pussy.

I had visited JS only once while he was still in the slammer. But this in itself was a revelation. I now knew what was the fate of college sophomores who stopped for burgers in soaking wet jeans just this side of the Rio Grande. That was how it had played out. JS and Roy—now long dead from an overdose so I guess I can use his name—had stashed the trash bag of pot in some bushes on the Mexican side, crossed over the border in their VW bug, and then waded back across the river to retrieve it. And then the hunger pangs and the burger joint along the highway. And then the waitress or whoever it was and the soaking wet jeans and the phone call to the Highway Patrol and the lockup in Del Rio. Clearly everyone within a mortar's heave of the border was on a sort of perpetual stakeout.

Karen was what my family would have called White Trash back then. I did not realize it at the time but her English was purported to be closer to Shakespeare's than my own. So much for the social distinctions of the suburban middle class. She was skinny in an Olive Oyl sort of way and had pale skin and jet black hair and moved a little jumpily the way a marionette moves. I could not figure out whether I was supposed to like her or not, though I did. The first time I took a piss in their trailer she came into the little bathroom and asked if I wanted her to shake it for me. I did but said I didn't. I don't think she was hurt. Except for the jumpiness she seemed without a doubt the most casual woman I had ever met in my life.

We dropped acid the first night I visited them in their trailer and Karen had what we used to call a Bum Trip. She sat in the open door of the trailer and stared at the woods across the dirt road and wept and shook and wept and shook. I think a fairy tale she had read when she was a kid had come back in full force. The trees, she kept repeating, immobilized, the trees are dark. JS fed her some downers to keep the pines from closing in and later on she came back inside and cleaned up her face. Thank god for that. I don't have the words to describe what she looked like when she was in the grip of her demons.

Later that night they went to bed and I prepared to sack out on the couch. It wasn't long before she came back into the little living room and asked if I wanted to join them in bed. She was wearing a very revealing negligee. I said No That's Okay or something to that effect. Then she made sure I did not miss out on anything and went back into the bedroom. Nothing was said about this in the morning. After breakfast JS went out for more drugs and I sat on the couch and watched the news on tv. The ROTC building on campus had burned down overnight and the National Guard had been called up. Karen was still in her negligee as she swiped the glass top of the coffee table in front of the couch. She bent over and I glimpsed what I had not been able to see the night before when she was only on top of me.

A couple years later I was in Boston for the summer on the lam from a busted relationship that I was certain was not my fault. A famous poet was teaching a special session at Harvard and I wanted to sit in on some first-hand insight into what the poetry world was up to and where it was going. The famous poet was a good guy and made sure the school did not try to hit us vagabond types up for tuition fees. JS and Karen drove up to Boston and the three of us headed out to the beach and hit some bars. JS and Karen disappeared for about an hour and when they came back to the car where I was stretched out on the back seat her eyes were blackened and her nose had been bloodied. Nothing was said about this. But it was clear in the stillness of the night that she still loved him and had not yet done their time together.

*

MASH NOTE TO THE DEA

When my father was diagnosed with a rare and incurable cancer I decided it was high time I packed up and spent some serious quality weeks with him back in Ohio. I was living overseas in Asia but the academic year at the school where I was teaching included two generous vacation periods.

I was past forty and my writing had never really gotten any traction. The publishing house that had brought out my first book went belly up a couple of months afterwards. Sadly one of the books on their list became a Hollywood hit a few years later. Even earned Nicholas Cage an Oscar, as I recall. Perhaps they could have made out on the paperback rights. But that's all water under the bridge. And I guess I should have been pleased that something with my name on the spine had a bar code on the back cover. Some people never even get that.

I was writing a story in my boyhood bedroom at my parents' house about a full blown schizophrenic who was carrying on a penpal relationship with a dirt poor Filipina who lived in a slum. It was an epistolary story—a story told in letters sent back and forth between the hapless nut job holed up in a flophouse in Cleveland and a girl I was basing on a freelancer I had shacked up with for a week after debarking the USS *Decatur* for good in Subic Bay.

The afternoon I was tying up the loose ends on the final draft my father knocked on my bedroom door. I invited him in and he stretched out on my bed and stared searchingly up at the ceiling. It was clear he had not shaved in a couple of days and this was unusual for him. He was a doctor who had spent twenty minutes scrubbing his hands every morning while I was growing up. Even on days when he did not go in to the office.

No sooner had he opened up than the tears began to flow. Yes it was true that he had retired after forty years of private practice because of the diagnosis. That was not what he had come to unburden himself about. The past year had been hell for him and not because he knew his days were numbered. Within days after he had taken down his shingle he had been arrested, charged and later convicted of distributing a controlled substance to a DEA plant posing as a patient. He spent a month in a Fed joint in Florida. Working in the infirmary, as I recall. Paid a hundred grand in fines. He had not seriously fought the charges because he wanted to keep it out of papers as much as possible–the grandchildren and all that. Naturally his medical license had been suspended. Of all the things this was what bothered him the most.

The plant was a woman who claimed she needed to lose weight and my father had a reputation for helping the obese shed pounds. He gave her a bottle of pills as a sort of gratis starter set and told her he would write her out a prescription for more when she came back in if the pills seemed to be doing any good. The bottle contained twice the legal limit a doctor can give a patient under such circumstances. This was the law. Or at least the new law that had come into effect some months earlier. This, at least, was his side of the story. He had not known the law had changed. His desk was a pile of unopened mail that last year of practice. Perhaps there was a registered letter in there from the Feds or the AMA. I do not know the other side of the story. The DEA plant's side. The sting side. I do wonder if she was packing heat in her purse when she visited my father's office. He was seventy years old the day he closed up shop. I wonder if she sobbed when she confessed to my father how unhappy she was to have such a fat ass and no decent social life at all. That sounds bitter now, I know, and is probably unfair. No doubt she had been told she was Fighting the Good Fight. And to give them their due, her handlers probably figured they had to swoop in before the slick old bastard gave them the slip out the cold door to the grave. Such are our tax dollars at work, I thought grimly. Such the career paths they blaze.

I consoled my father as best I could. Hugged him and told him I loved him, which had always been more or less the truth. Then he said something that shocked me. He apologized for slapping me when I denied plagiarizing a composition I had handed in to my seventh grade English teacher. I had turned in the little masterpiece on gazing at a mountain peak and gotten it back with an A+ at the top that was crossed out and a vicious accusation penciled in next to it. I was ordered to march to the front of the class and Young Mrs. Grundy repeated the accusation to everyone in the room. It was my first month of junior high and many of my classmates' faces were new to me and naturally I burst into tears as I adamantly refused to confess. Her ferocity that afternoon was incomprehensible to me. It was soon cruelly whispered about that she was an unhappy woman with a miscarriage or two under her belt and I think the miserable wretch read every book and magazine article in the school library about climbing Mt. Everest to try to nail me after the fact. Weeks went by and no apology forthcame. But it was a relief to let it slide. And the other kids in the class had taken my side from the beginning. In the end that's all you ever really need if you are a kid. I don't think it ever dawned on her that you could make up a good story just by watching a program on television about trekking the Himalayas or listening to one on the radio. I don't think she understood that it could actually be fun to make something up and use your own words to do it. In a crazy sort of way to this day I count her among my darker muses.

And the crazier thing was that my father had never smacked me. Ever. Not for denying I had plagiarized a stupid composition assignment. Not for anything else. He had growled a little that evening, sure, and then listened patiently to my whining and indignant protestations of innocence. But years later he had misremembered the whole episode. I don't know why. What warped his memory. The terminal cancer diagnosis. The radiation and then the chemo. The lost cause he knew it was. The DEA. Your guess is as good as mine.

When I published my first poems as a grad student he purchased fifty copies of that issue of *The North American Review*. I did not know about this at the time. I found them in a box when I was cleaning up the basement after his death. Yep, there they were, the poems: "Diplomatique" and "Pumping Ethyl."

After his death my mother told me that the only people who called up to register their moral support after his arrest were his Black patients. Not the Hungarians. Not the Poles. Not the house calls in Little Italy. And he had had plenty of those. Loads of them from the Old Country. Refugees and the children of refugees from the Nazis and the Reds and whatever else oppressed people back in the old days. They had worshipped him once and patted my head when I was a kid and asked if I wanted to grow up to be a family doctor like my old man. But they were comfortable now in America and obeyed its rules.

After my father got up off the bed and shambled out the room, I finished up my story about the horny schizophrenic former high school teacher—named Harold Nitcombe III, I don't know why—and the dirt poor Filipina I had based on a girl I had shacked up with in Manila for a week so many years before. Her name was Josie. The free-lancer, I mean. I remember that. She wept and shook and wept and shook when I slipped her the envelope before getting into the taxi for the airport. I remember that, too. And the taste of her tears.

*

REPLY TO ALL

Gang,

I'm going to keep this short as I can—it's near midnight now and I need some sleep. First, for those of you young-sters not yet contacted by the City's Finest, here's a taste of what you might have to look forward to: Three plain-clothes detectives visited my office at school around 3 PM today, asked if I had been involved in Babo Palooza, told me that if so I had violated two Korean laws, to wit 1) participating in a public performance not approved by the Ministry of Culture & Harassment and 2) engaging in a an activity outside the approved parameters of my visa status, and requested that I come down to the station near City Hall by 7 PM.

At the Police Station I ran into Conrad and we were

able to chat for a few minutes before being separated for our interviews. I'm sure he will have a lot to say soon. He was still being interviewed when I was let go about 10 PM. (That's right–they grilled me for nigh onto 3 hours.) I'll try to condense what I learned here. But first let me note that that the cop was very polite, even affable, concerned about my "rights," and provided me with an interpreter who was not–he emphasized–employed by the police–a grad student in English at Gobuksan University of Foreign Studies, in fact. She had never dealt with a foreigner criminal before–it was her first time inside a police station, I gathered–but she did her best.

His first question was whether I had ever been in trouble with the authorities in Korea before. I decided to play it straight and fessed up to a tiff over the number of "ladies' drinks" on a Texas Street bar bill that attracted the attention of a brace of patrolling coppers. This was wise on my part as he noted he already had that down in my case file. Of course he could have been bluffing–or not. His desk was cluttered and I could get no more than a glimpse at anything on it.

To cut to the chase, the police were most interested in the organization known as About Face Theater and especially the cover of the Babo Palooza program and the names on it. He leaned on me a little as to the significance of "Babo Palooza". He seemed to grok that Babo means "fool" in Korean (duh) but Palooza had him stumped and I wasn't much in the mood to help him there. (Crazily the whole "Babo" business kept reminding me of a bizarro triad in a famous Melville story. Google Benito Cereno if you are of a literary bent.) He wanted to know who the capo was–Andy or Peter. I said we really didn't have one and that About Face was mostly a bunch of young (except obviously for me) writer/actor/stand-up comedian expats sitting around a bar drinking beer and pooling ideas for a Show. Gradually it became clear that indeed we had broken a law by performing publicly without permission from the Authorities–and that by charging admission AND distributing half a cooler of cheap local beer we had compounded our crime. I told them (cop and interpreter) that the admission fee and beer were sort of afterthoughts and that we had neither made money nor intended to. This did not tip the balance in our favor, as far as I could see. The performance was the violation, not the money, according to cop via interpreter. He also asked a lot of questions about how deeply involved I was in the show, who invited me (sorry Peter) to do my Steam Irons of De-sire monologue routine, how long I had known Andy and Peter, etc. The cop also asked a lot of questions about re-hearsals–the "organization" thing again. It was difficult to tell how much he knew and he had told me I would have to sign the statement (the interview transcript, that is) at the end so I didn't want to get caught in an out and out fib. This may be where they are planning to nail people: organization, planning, rehearsals etc., so I tried to play up the spontaneity aspect of things, but I don't think he bought into that too much. Point: the cops had been tipped off. Clearly our rehearsals in the big gym at the univ had been staked out. For all intents and purposes, the plainclothesman–or more likely plainclotheswoman—in the audience that night was part of a Sting. Make no mistake about that.

After the official interview was over we went "off the record." The cop said it wasn't nice to make fun of other cultures–though throughout the evening I had tried to make clear that the show made fun of us Westerners more than our illustrious hosts–but irony (and explaining it) was not my interpreter's strong suit. I did a lot of humble hand-wringing throughout all this as if agonizing over our thoughtless rudenesses. The cop then told me that when he went to "America" for Police Department Clinical Observation Training (or whatever–this kind of got lost in translation) he saw Americans cheating on their wives all over the place and Korean husbands did not do such things, but he would never make fun of Westerners for our immoral practices. (Was he hanging out with Drew Peterson in Chicago or what? Makes one wonder.) At one point he used the expression "way-gook-nom" and when the interpreter winced he quickly caught himself and amended it to "way-gook-in." (For you neophytes in the loop, "way-gook-nom" translates roughly as Piece of Shit Foreigner and "way-gook-in" is nicer, whatever that may be.) At the end of the evening, besides signing the statement that everything was true to the best of my knowledge, I was fingerprinted and asked to sign a waiver that I did not request them to notify my embassy that I had been detained. Hard to tell how serious all this is, but better eat a big meal

Before You Go In,
B.

PART THREE:
OTHERWHERES

He felt a sense of delicious expectation, the anticipation of a chemist almost at the end of a long sequence, when the colorless liquids may at last be mixed and begin to blush with color, slowly but steadily brightening now like an annunciation . . .

William T. Vollmann
Whores for Gloria

PUMPING ETHYL

I dreamed we could get married
in any gas station in America
between the gumball and cigarette machines

while the preacher stood on the hydraulic lift

going up as slow as yeast
and down the hiss of compressed
air as organist

with the little numbers on the pumps
flipping back into their sockets

like drunken friends

at the reception

when all the cake is gone

THE INITIATION STORY
A HISTORY OF MY
AUTO EROTICISM

Back in the mid-50's when I was still a preschooler my older sister or one of the other bigger kids in the neighborhood would walk me to the end of the block and we would stand there on the corner as the traffic whizzed up and down the main drag. My job was to name the name of each car as it approached and zipped past: *Caddy-lack, Hudson, DeSoto, Ford, Chevy.* My older sister or Nancy Fisher or Mary Margaret Kovach—it was always an older girl, come to think of it—deemed it a stunning feat of the intellect that a toddler who could not yet recite his ABC's was able to name any and all of the multitude of automobile makes that jockeyed for consumer approbation in those optimistic, halcyon days of mid-century America: *Cry-slur, Nash, Mercury, Kaiser, Stoody-baker.*

For me, of course, the front ends of those cars were simply familiar faces: chromium grill mouths, glassy headlight eyes, haughty hood ornament noses, and beneath each hood ornament nose a shiny heraldic emblem like a tiny Hitler moustache. I knew them the way I knew the names and faces of my brothers and sisters and cousins and aunts and uncles and neighbors and the puppets and their more human interlocutors on Saturday morning television: Buffalo Bob Smith and Fran Allison and Uncle Andy Devine. I never claimed any originality in this. There were plenty of children's books and movie matinee cartoons depicting wheezy, out-of-breath automobiles sagging on deflated tires like tired hound dogs at the end of an uphill chase, distending from their front-end grillwork flat, pink, throbbing, exhausted tongues. If each brand of automobile had its own personality—its own character—in my imagination, I don't remember. All I know is what I've been told over the years: that you just had to tell me the name of a car one time and I would know it, remember it, for good. I could not tell you today what a '53 Kaiser looked like back then, but I believe if I saw one this afternoon I would recognize it. It was that kind of thing.

Naturally as the months and then years passed the charm of marching me down the block to show off my mnemonic skills wore off. A four-year-old prodigy is one thing, but a semi-bright nine-year-old can name more things under the bloody sun—baseball pitchers, Confederate regiments at Gettysburg, reptiles—than anybody ever wants to hear about. Sometimes on that very same corner of Oxford and Noble Roads my sister would grab one of my fourth-grade classmates in whom I had lately expressed interest and hold her in a bear hug whilst I like a pinfeathered raptor pecked mercilessly at the poor girl's blushing cheek with what I was convinced were passionate kisses, but that was the extent of the enthusiasm older sister Janet had in watching me perform there. Had she only known.

In junior high it all went into a kind of reverse. Numbers were the name of Mnemosyne's game there, and she was a harsh mistress. Speak not to me of algebraic equations. I had difficulty memorizing simple digits, particularly the combination of the lock on my locker. My homeroom teacher would find me standing in the hall after the bell had rung, standing there and staring at the face of the lock with its sixty-odd calibrations and the forlorn arrow which had no idea which way to turn or what numbers to stop at. It was an unnerving blank to draw. Miss Townsend would lay a weary palm on my shoulder like an overtasked muse and call me her "Li'l Alzheimer" and flip through a sheaf of papers on her clipboard and announce: Right 22-Left 49-Right 6. Of course I'm making them up now. I have no idea what those numbers were, obviously never did. But the front end of a '53 Kaiser . . .

And then high school. And lists, endless lists of lists. *30 Days to a More Powerful Vocabulary.* The Amendments to the Constitution. The Periodic Table. Sines and cosines

and tangents and cotangents and secants and cosecants.
First, second and third declension Latin nouns. *Puella,
puellae, puellarum, puellas.* Girls. Girls in the nomina-
tive, in the genitive, in the dative, in the accusative cases.
Objects of prepositions. Propositions. Of verbs: *Osculo.*
Girls. Kiss. I kiss. I kiss girls. I tried, failed, without older sister Janet there to hold their arms pinned back for
me. And then one Friday night after the dance, a breach,
a breakthrough. A deep wet exchange that left my gums
tingling, my uvula ablaze. We called them French kisses
in those days, never having heard of the real McCoy, that
rooting down there at drainage beneath the grassy knoll.
That came later, in college—or, as in my case, during a
brief stint in hippiedom and then a hitch with Uncle Sam.

But red-headed Cheryl M. was that first one of mine.
Friday nights, Saturday nights, even the odd school night,
we slurped and slobbered and swiped and smeared each
others' faces—if it began with an "s" and even just connot-
ed wetness, we did it—in the privacy of her family's rec
room. We smooched till our lips stung and the braces that
were guiding her teeth with glacial slowness into align-
ment dug into the tender flesh inside her mouth and she
bled. Cheryl, sadly, was a harelip—I didn't run with the
jock and cheerleader crowd—and that Saturday evening
as the blood oozed along the silver wire that corralled her

tilted, staccato choppers it dawned on me that she looked exactly like the crushed front end of an orange '52 Buick I had witnessed careen headlong into a utility pole.

After that night, I couldn't shake the impression. Every time I looked at her red hair and that ruined mouth, I saw the stoved in grillwork of that orange Buick, the radiator flooding the asphalt with pink engine coolant. I couldn't tell her this, of course. She was a sensitive one. But the frequency of our immersions into osculatory abandon dropped off dramatically—until she emerged from the hospital during summer vacation with a considerably improved upper lip. Forgive me if I confess that at the time I could not help surrendering to the fantasy of that '52 Buick rolling out of a body shop with a fresh coat of orange paint and a jubilant, if just ever so defiant, grin on its kisser.

That summer I pumped gas at the Sohio station on the corner of Mayfield and Coventry, the principal intersection in an enclave of aged Old World Jews slowly being infiltrated by long-haired headshop proprietors and their impecunious hippie clientele. In those days a pump jockey was something more than just a female cashier inside a bulletproof glass booth. When I handed you back your credit card receipt you got not only my initials in the corner but like as not my official thumbprint in fouled SAE

30-weight on top of the red, white and blue company logo, like a postmark on a postage stamp. In between customers I puttered about under the hydraulic lift, draining sumps and feeling up inside the wheelwells for the steel nipples of the lube fittings, peeling off the dried, caked grease—the color and consistency of coagulated umbilical blood, I recall, my older sister having delivered the first of her squalling brood earlier that spring—and securing the nozzle of the grease gun snug over the nipple and giving the trigger one or two steady pulls as the rubber seal swelled with the thick, rich lubricant. "Black mayonnaise," Cameron called it once, wolfing down half a baloney sandwich in two ravenous bites. "Phlegm of the devil," countered Old Ernie, hacking up a loogie. To me, though I made no contribution to the persiflage, it was disturbingly sexy stuff.

When a car pulled up to a pump island, Cameron, Old Ernie and I would pause and stare at each other. Whoever was not ruminating a bolus of jelly doughnut nor sucking the tar out of a Tiparillo would take the hike across the shimmering July griddle of concrete apron and service the customer. If it was the Shaker Heights blond in the classic '57 mocha T-Bird convertible with the chrome Continental kit, Cameron and I would stage a slapstick routine as we shouldered up against each other on our way out the door, vying to be the first to snatch the squeegee from atop the Boron pump and thereby garner the consecrate privilege of doing her windshield. Mini-skirts were in fashion that year, and Miss Clairol didn't wear panties in the summer months. Miss Clairol, yes, for the thatchwork on her beaver was jet as obsidian. The first time I strained for a chance glimpse of it through the glare of the windshield, I thought she was harboring a pet tarantula down there.

Miss Clairol came in twice a month that summer, but never predictably, and as often as not either Cameron or I would be caught flatfooted and diddling with the underside of some huge gas-guzzling beast up on the hydraulic lift when the mocha '57 T-Bird rolled up to a pump island. One afternoon out of the corner of my eye I caught Cameron streaking toward the Mayfield Road pumps. The T-Bird was sitting there with the top down under a scorching Ohio August sun and Cameron was at her pleasure in a flash, polishing the bugs off her headlights and drawing the squeegee ever so slowly across her windshield as he leered through the glass. I was in the lube bay under a '62 Mercury Montclair with my finger in the filler hole of the rear-end differential to check the level of grease. You put your finger in and pulled it out and if the underside came out coated black and slick then the reservoir was topped up fine.

That afternoon a wave of envy and rage swept over me as I stood there with an index finger the color of pitch and watched Cameron standing over the topless convertible and filling out the credit card receipt as he gorged his fantasy with unobstructed glances down past the steering column and into our shared cornucopia of imagined delights. Cameron's jaw was working overtime and at that moment Miss Clairol was gazing up at him with that expression of feigned interest and puzzled bemusement rich people will occasionally bestow on a menial.

I swiped off my finger on my jeans and made to saunter over and catch at the least the tail end of the transaction. I was barely out from under the Merc when Old Ernie barked at me and pointed to a green Lark pulled up alongside the Coventry Road pump island.

"Axel! It's that bitch Mrs. Wiesenberg! *You* do her! I want none of her window pecking!"

Old Ernie was a Jew-hating Pole with phlebitis in both legs who lined his leaky boots with plastic Wonder Bread wrappers on rainy days and kept three brand-new pairs of boots in the trunk of his Plymouth. I didn't know that much about Jews back then, except that they ate special, clean foods like haggis and filtered fish and wrote the first half of the Bible, the parts with all the voluptuous seductresses and noble studs like Judah Ben Hur, and that for some reason a teenager named Anne Frank had to pay for it all. And the first movie I ever took a girl to was *Judgment at Nuremburg*, which was a big mistake romantically speaking, the images were that hard to put into words over a milkshake on the walk home.

Old Ernie and Mrs. Esther Wiesenberg went at it every time he waited on her. She was a sour-breathed septuagenarian without a husband but with a tiny airhole in the glass of her Lark windshield that everyone save Mrs. Esther Wiesenberg agreed was a tiny airhole. She was certain it was a speck of road dirt, and every other Thursday at precisely three in the afternoon after her fill-up she demanded that Cameron or Old Ernie or Bill or whoever was manning the island remove it from her sight. It bothered her when she drove at night, she said. She sometimes mistook it for a "creature" in her path. It wasn't an airhole because an airhole would be an imperfection and the windshield of her Lark had no imperfections. The car had been presented to her by her nephew the ophthalmologist and he would not have given her a car with an imperfection in the glass. It was that simple, and it didn't pay to argue with a person of her obdurate will. You just rubbed at it for a requisite full five minutes until on cue someone inside the station hailed you in to take a call on a pay phone that had not rung. Cameron was waving goodbye to Miss Clairol as I shot him the dirtiest look I could muster and walked over to the green Lark idling impatiently at the Coventry Road pumps.

Mrs. Wiesenberg began pecking and scratching at the airhole before I had even finished filling her tank. The airhole was a couple inches above her Jewish Community Center parking permit decal and I couldn't see it unless I got up real close and found an angle that didn't reflect the sunglare back into my face. In the heat Mrs. W. had loosened the cuffs of her prim blouse and as she lifted an arm to resume pecking at the glass, her sleeve slid down to her elbow, revealing the saggy, grayish, liver-spotted skin of a cross old woman. And a faded blue serial number tattooed into the flesh of her forearm.

I don't know if my jaw dropped, or my eyes bulged. I tried not to look away, and then I tried to look like I hadn't noticed anything out of the norm. Mrs. W. continued to peck and scratch, peck and scratch, and I rubbed away at the "spot" with my cloth in a kind of lapidary frenzy, avoiding her eyes and the sight of the faded blue serial number tattooed to a forearm that seemed to have reached straight out of hell, like the hand scratching the handwriting on the wall in *The Ten Commandments: Mean,*

Mean, Tickle . . . something. A message from an Other Side, screened off from us mere mortal grinds by the gritty particulars of daily life that tick like bugs against our eyeballs—and the fond, laughable, vain, and absolutely sincere hope that Miss Clairol and her mocha T-Bird from heaven with its cargo of bliss would appear when I had the jump on Cameron and spirit me away with her to some remote and exotic world of scented joss sticks and paper-thin walls behind which everything imaginable was done in the buff.

"You are not going to tell me that's an airhole in the glass, are you, young man?"

"Nome," I answered.

"But it's not an airhole, is it, young man?"

"I don't quite know what it is, ma'am."

I had already told her it was an airhole on half a dozen occasions. As had Cameron. As had Old Ernie.

"Is that dear man William working today?"

"Bill's off this week. Vacation, ma'am."

"I should have known. When you people don't know something you just say it's an airhole. You don't know," she snapped wearily, and put the little Lark in gear and maneuvered her way from the pump island back into the traffic on Coventry Road.

Back inside the station Cameron sat on the high stool

with a shit-eating grin plastered across his face like a bill-
board advertising dental resurrection.

"You would not believe it, Axel. You will NOT believe
this."

"Don't even try me, Cameron."

"It was incredible."

"I'm sure it was."

"I just saw something I've never seen before in my entire life."

"Miss Clairol in the T-Bird. I know all about it. Lucky
you."

"She asked me . . ."

"I think I just told you I don't want to hear about it."

"That old lady really put a burr up your ass, huh?
Well, listen. Miss Clairol asked me if I thought she was a
natural blond."

"Really," I said. "And I suppose you told her she was
another Anita Ekberg."

"And then she hiked up her skirt and spread her thighs
just so. Like she always does."

"I've seen it," I said with the inflated disdain of a new-
found worldliness. "Four times."

"No, man. No. She dyed it. She dyed the fucking thing
BLOND!"

"You're kidding," I gasped. I was seventeen. That June,

Cheryl M. and I had seen a flick at the drive-in in which a Nazi *Oberfuhrer* had lifted the back of Ekberg's skirt with a riding crop and gotten a good look at her blackmarket drawers. "Wow, man. What did you say?"

"I couldn't say anything at first. I was stumped speech-less."

"Yeah . . . and?"

"Well, of course I know a rich private college girl like Miss Clairol isn't going to have anything to do with me. Or some high school putz like you. She's just fucking with our heads with those beaver shots. I know that, man."

"Of course," I said. Though I hadn't really thought about it that way, at least until Cameron came right out and put it into words.

"Right on, man. Of course. So I drew myself up and smiled and gaped right down at her little nest of bleached yarn and said, 'Ma'am, when a woman reveals a bit of her intimate self to a man, I suppose he's liable to tell her any-thing he thinks she wants to hear.' "

"Christ! What did *she* say?"

"Nothing! She just laughed. She thought it was great!"

"Damn," I said as Ernie hobbled out of the stockroom with a couple of spools of elastic supporter and headed for the men's room to rewrap his phlebitic legs.

"Axel," he barked as he passed me. "That old Jew bitch give you any crap about her goddam airhole?"

"No, sir," I said. "Just the usual."

"Well, just don't go telling her no lies that it ain't a airhole like Bill sometimes does. Nobody has to be nice to everybody all the time."

"We call 'em as we see 'em, Ern," Cameron laughed, infinitely pleased with himself.

"Ernie," I said, but the old piss had already passed into the men's room and shot the bolt on the door.

"Hot damn," Cameron roared and turned and rapped a brisk tattoo on the shelf of roadmaps behind the high stool. "I saw it! Wait till I get back to State and tell the guys about this! She dyed it, man. She dyed it BLOND! And I saw it!"

"Do you want to hear what I just saw?" I offered meekly.

But Cameron had already sprung from the stool to wait on a rickety VW bus emblazoned with Day-Glo peace symbols that had pulled up to the Mayfield island pumps. It was full of hippie chicks with electrified hair, ornaments the size of piston rings dangling from their ears and, no doubt, fretted holes in strategic places on their jeans. And Cameron had gotten the jump on me again.

With the last days of my senior year came the prom. Flame-haired Cheryl M. consented to go with me, though with her new upper lip she had managed to nibble her way from obscure outcast status at school to the veritable fringes of popularity and thus a bit closer to its feverish, molten, in-crowd core. She had two other offers, in fact, but I was a sentimental favorite and won the day when I fessed up about the orange '52 Buick and her former smile. She respected my honesty, she said. And I had cared for her in her previous, unfortunate old-self incarnation, though a corollary truth that I did not own up to was the fact that she had been the only girl I could ever get to sit down next to me on a sofa. And besides, neither of the two other offers tendered was the blow-bag captain of the school debate team, whom she in turn fessed up to be holding out for.

The theme of the prom that year was "3 Deuces and a 4-Speed and a 389" and the music The Beach Boys and Jan and Dean and Ronnie and the Daytonas. In those days my father drove a white second-hand Valiant V-6 that looked like it had been designed in an Italian bakery, so I emptied my bank account—I wasn't college-bound, anyhow, with my old man on strike half the year round—and rented a navy blue Pontiac GTO automatic that could lay a thirty-foot patch of rubber if you gunned the engine and dropped it from neutral into drive. Eight cylinders of pure, unadulterated automotive lust. I figured with it being prom night and all, there was a fair chance that Cheryl and I might get down to something heavier than merely sucking heads, and I wanted to improve the odds. Underneath the front seat I had secreted a pint bottle of vodka, a quart of o.j., and a brace of paper cups. After the dance the in-crowd took a midnight cruise down the Cuyahoga on the *Goodtimes II* with a dance band and mixers and ice supplied. We lesser mortals were left to fend for ourselves, me in a rented incarnadine Dino Martin tuxedo jacket that smelled faintly of cleaning fluid and Cheryl in a blue chiffon evening dress that made about four different swishy sounds depending upon which limb she chose to stir. After pizza and Cokes with her best friend Genevieve—a doomed, waif-like creature undergoing chemo and sporting a pitiful straw-colored wig that looked like it had been elicited from the obscure recesses of a broom closet—and her escort Warren the Mooch, we ended up in the back seat of the GTO parked in the shadow of a wing of the first elementary school we could find. I mixed up a couple of lukewarm screwdrivers in the paper cups and we threw the first round down, and a second, and a third. And soon enough, naturally, the tears began to roll.

"You've been so-o-o good to me, Axel," she wept.

"No, I haven't."

"Yes you have," she insisted and began to laugh maniacally through the lacrimal mist. "So *honest*."

"Not really," I said, basking in the flattery.

"No, Axel. No. It's really true. You have always been the most honestest person I know."

She gave me a gentle poke in the sternum with a forefinger for emphasis as her mood of maniacal laughter melted into one of double superlative baby-talk giddiness.

"Most honestest! Hee hee hee! Did I really say *that*?"

And then from giddiness to utter sincerity:

"Axel, I want you to know you can tell me *anything*. Ask me *anything*."

And from utter sincerity to inflamed lust as she got up on her knees on the back seat and performed a jaunty sequence of sinuous pelvic grinds:

"Let's do it, Axel. Let's do it tonight. Fuck the world! Fuck them all! All those cocksuckers who made fun of my harelip."

I sat back in stunned silence. And not because of the "let's do it" part. I just had never heard her use the word "harelip" before. Or "cocksucker," for that matter.

"Anything you want, Axel. Anything you want."

And again the tears began to roll. We had come full circle.

"Anything, Axel. Anything anything anything anything."

"Well . . ." I said.

"Anything!"

"I guess we could do it," I said. It seemed like she was changing her moods awfully fast.

"Anything," she cooed and gave my arm a tug, spilling the dregs of my screwdriver round four into a fold of my cummerbund.

"Well, I never thought I could tell you this, but . . ."

"Okay. Okay okay okay okay."

". . . I'd really like to see your muff."

"WHAT?"

"I mean, is it the same red color . . ."

"WHAT?"

". . . as your head hair or . . ."

"WHAT THE HELL DO YOU TAKE ME FOR? SOME KIND OF GODDAM WHORE?"

"You said I could . . ."

She shoved forward the back of the front seat, flipped the door handle and sprang from the GTO. I watched her stumble and fall on the parking lot blacktop and get up again and brush herself off. She spun around once and looked up at the sky as if searching the stars for a witness to her humiliation. I got out of the car and begged her to get back in. I had only been kidding, I didn't really want her to show . . .

"*You* get back in the car, you sonuvabitch! Axel, *you* get back in the car!"

I begged again, pleaded. We were in a quiet neighborhood. Beyond the school playground a few lights still burned in a row of squat one-story bungalows.

"Get back in, Axel. Get back in behind the wheel. I'll show you what you wanna see!"

I got back in and Cheryl moved off until she was some twenty yards in front of the GTO.

"TURN ON THE FUCKING LIGHTS, AX-HOLE!"

I tugged the switch and the parking lot flooded with an unearthly, pallid glare. She looked tiny, standing there, her blue chiffon dress shredded about the knees.

"GIVE ME THE FUCKING BRIGHTS!"

I gave the switch another tug and ratcheted up the candlepower a full dimension. She put her forearm up in front of her eyes and then put it down.

"OKAY."

And then the dress was up over her head and off.

"YOU PEOPLE! ALWAYS WANTING TO STARE! ALWAYS WANTING TO LOOK!"

She curled her upper lip and froze the snarl and pooched her chin forward defiantly.

And then her panties and nylons were down about her ankles. And off. Kicked up into the air. I didn't bother to follow where they had fallen. She stood there naked from her bra on down, in the beams of the headlights her bush no more than a flyspeck, a fleck, a mote. I leaned forward and rested my chin on the steering wheel and squinted through the windshield.

"COME ON! GET CLOSER! DON'T YOU WANT A GOOD LOOK!"

I switched on the ignition, put the GTO in gear, and inched forward. And that was when it sort of swam into view, the airhole in the glass of the windshield, in a direct line of sight from me to Cheryl's tiny muff, like the bead of a gunsight. And I knew at that moment if I put my foot down on the accelerator, punched it, I could bring to an end something dark and cruel and strange. For her, and maybe for the both of us. I let the GTO creep nearer.

"COME ON, AX-HOLE!   YOU KNOW WHAT YOU WANT!"

Nobody really believed either of us, because we didn't tell anybody the whole truth. Not the two cops in the squad car that screeched to a halt just as I had the grill of the GTO breathing a few inches from Cheryl's divine fiery shrub. Not Cheryl's parents, who grudgingly dropped the charges against me after they took her to a ladies' doctor and later a shrink and found that she was equally grudgingly *intacta*. Not my own folks, who heard a third version of the story, the most artful and therefore the flimsiest and fakest of the lot, though they hardly cared, being parents of a son. Not the whole truth. Not the part about the hard-on anyways, and how I was able to tuck it back inside my tuxedo trousers just in time. Not about the jerked-off come and the spilled lukewarm screwdriver all mixed up in the folds of my cummerbund. Not the whole truth. But that was okay. Because, look at it this way, people are happy to hear lies, and if you want to get anywhere with anybody, you've got to tell them what they want to hear.

THE TALE
MY FIRST FOREIGN WOMAN
AND THE SEA

There was a blind woman who fell in love with a stout sailor from a distant land. He was a good man and did not touch her, though she wished him to, in her heart. He was a stranger to her city, but he took her out to various eating houses and described for her blind eyes the rainbow colors of the food set on the table before them. But it was an exotic culture to him and the hues were subtle and beyond his range of language, for the blind woman and the sailor spoke to each other only haltingly in a crude lingua franca.

Sometimes they returned together to her narrow room above the seamstress shop where she made her living stuffing scraps of cloth into pillows for the rich. He drank beer there and snacked on the dried fish and dark sausages that she prepared for him from memory. The sailor was a fat man, a man of the gut, and did his thinking and feeling down there in the labyrinth of the guts. He broke wind one evening, leaning close to her as he provided a sluice for the gas to escape. (You know what I mean.) The blind woman smiled and he saw her smile. "What was that?" she asked, knowing full well. "That is the sound of a man who loves you, when he is near," he answered. The blind woman liked the pure idea of the sentiment and invited him to lie down with her. He followed, both thinking: *What is there to lose?*

But he was a sailor from a foreign land and soon would be gone. This bothered her, of course. He would be gone, perhaps forever. She would miss him and his flatulence that announced, in its abrupt clarion way, the making of love. So she pursed her lips and began practicing explodents and susurras against her encroaching abandonment. She mastered the squeal and the thundering bassoon. As the final day grew near, she cooked up a good pot of red beans for him, the kind packed with molecules of blue methane aching for release.

On his last night in port he climbed the creaky stairs to her room and she fed him well, spooning the purplish mash in the direction of his mouth with mother love. Giddy, he began to break wind like there was no tomorrow, which there wasn't. She followed his lead, blindly, matching him vibration for vibration with her practiced lips. He was a breezy old sea-dog and taught her more in that last evening than any landlocked blighter could ever hope to know.

Then he sailed. A storm rose out of the east, his hermaphrodite brig splintered and sank, all drowned. Perhaps a pool of bubbles gamboled on the surface of the ocean for a moment, she thought when she heard the report. But she had learned her lessons well and recited them over and over in her room. Phoo-oo-oot. Phleesh. Shuh-kuh-kuh. Vleen. Brap. High-pitched farts and low-pitched farts and farts that tromboned in between. Sometimes she forgot herself and left her window open. A blind woman living alone in a room above a seamstress shop doesn't much care what the neighbors think.

I too was a sailor, in my youth, and had heard all the tales about foreign port cities young sailors hear on their first voyages. One evening, while the rest of the crew luxuriated in the local fleshpots, I stood in front of a seamstress shop leaning against a wall, a Players dangling from my lips, a tableau of solitude and dreams adrift. The strange and foreign port city at night was ablaze with torchlights in its cocky, smirky way, as foreign port cities always are. It was then that I heard him, above me, a sound I had listened to a hundred times late at night when the Dansker and Jenkins and Kincaid squatted and plotted in the lee forechains drinking watered rum and dicing away their pay: the song of the legendary Drowned Farter. (It was said a pool of bubbles gamboled perpetually on the surface of the ocean at the exact spot his ship went down.) This, of course, was Adventure. I climbed the creaky stairs and entered the blind woman's room. She sat cross-legged on a mound of rich pillows at the center of a web of ghostly threads connecting her fingertips to various corners of the room, like rigging on a ship, her haunted blind eyes long ago emptied of longing, a weathered figurehead on a bowsprit.

But she was kind and understood my loneliness. She took me slowly, knowing that I was young and that my heart was crowded with all the useless baby furniture of young hope. On her pillows farts exploded overhead like rockets, rattled below like grapeshot at the waterline. Ripped and snapped like sails in a gale, canvas that billowed and sagged and filled again. Hot musket breath raked the poop. I boarded her. She boarded me. And when she pulled me under for the third time and I felt my brief life spent before me in a few seconds, I was grateful for the foretaste.

You never forget her, your first foreign woman in a port city, regardless of the men she's had ahead of you or will have later on. You board your ship the next morning and when the wind kicks up you want to turn back. Standing on the wooden deck you see your first foreign woman's blind eyes in your own mind's eye, and then you hear the crew scrambling up the ratline rungs of the shrouds, stinking of last night's beer, farting their early morning farts and singing in chorus of their own first foreign women and the sea.

THE TALL DAHL TALE
THE ASSASSIN AND THE GYPSY

The Mexican tour had not been a success. The star performers had had to wear white sequined-spangled costumes in order to show up under the weak lights, and the brown stains on the seats of their pants forced them to walk around stiffly upright, sucking in their rear ends as they moved. The lion tamer could not fool the lions, who got their claws tangled in the rungs of his chair just to make him bend over. The clowns tie-dyed their baggy clown suits Aztec chocolate to disguise the effects of the dysentery. The fine ladies who stood on the backs of the white horses as they pranced in circles in the center ring had stitched fluffy white bunny tails at strategic spots under their tutus.

The trapeze artist had a more sweeping solution: he hired an assassin. This would be his last tour. It wasn't just the cramps and stains that bothered him, but also the beans with hot peppers they had been eating for weeks. Every time he went into a downswing the thrust of the beans and peppers coupled with the flatufacient medicine he was taking propelled him forward at a velocity he was unused to, and he kept coming closer to speeding past the outstretched hands of his brother. Sooner or later he would miss the connection and his name would be added to the sad annals of Circus History's failures. He instructed the assassin to shoot him in the belly, right below the navel, as soon as he had completed his warm up swings and was back at the top of his arc, ready to swoop down again to make the exchange. It was here that he felt most angelic, most ready to die.

He told the assassin to shoot him in the stomach at exactly that moment when all the volatile gases in his system had gathered in one place in a single knot. The assassin would know this moment by the squinched expression on the trapeze artist's face. The bullet would puncture his abdomen and there would be a fireball, as in the detonation of an outhouse packed with TNT. The body would disintegrate so quickly that all that remained would be a tiny flake of skin, floating down like a feather. This was how the trapeze artist saw it, and the assassin did not gainsay him.

The assassin took aim from a back row seat. The trapeze artist completed his warm up swings and arched his back as if about to drop into the first exchange. When the bullet struck home there was a tremendous explosion. Threads of abdominal wall and bits of dark matter hung suspended in the air for a moment and then filtered down upon the upturned faces of the amazed and delighted

Mexican children. Never on any feast day had they seen such a thing.

The Mexican children thought that the trapeze artist was a new kind of *piñata*, which is a hollow effigy suspended over the blindfolded head of a *niño* or *niña* at a *cumpleaños* party. The birthday child swings wildly at it with a stick that sooner or later connects and a cloudburst of candy and toys rains down upon the squealing throng.

Hungrily the children scavenged for the shreds of innards and gooey pellets of human waste, greedily stuffing their mouths whenever they were able to come up with something.

Their parents didn't mind. After all, it was a *circus*. And a circus is a kind of *carnaval*.

There was a gypsy woman in the circus who told fortunes in her Gypsy wagon just behind the exhibit of Old World hyenas. This was not at all such a bad allotment in the circus' pecking order, to her mind. The hyenas' nightly harmonizings crooned her to sleep each evening and filled her dreams with strange and unnatural cravings, which she could only assuage with generous midnight applications of grilled cheese sandwiches.

So the Gypsy woman was of a passionate, suggestive nature and she had long loved the trapeze artist from afar, and when she heard the assassin's shot ring out and the subsequent explosion she rushed to the entrance of the big top and saw the Mexican children swarming there like ants. She looked up at the trapeze, from which dangled something both ominous and obscene.

Now the Gypsy woman was an augur, and in the days before crystal balls and Christ Our Savior her ancestors had been adept at reading truth from the spilled guts of animals, even humans, in true *haruspex* fashion. But a wrist-thick length of pallid, blood-speckled intestine dangling like a dead worm from a trapeze above a mob of frenzied, incredulous Mexican children: *What could that forbode?*

She closed her eyes in order to let the visions come more fluidly. At once she was knocked on her can by someone rushing past her. She opened her eyes and saw a man with a rifle running between the legs of a string of elephants that were standing at the entrance of the tent awaiting their cue. The man fell once, and his face went *splat!* into a coconut-sized ball of elephant dung, but he recovered quickly and fled into the distance.

The Gypsy woman, true to her Gypsy nature, interpreted this event as a sign, a hint of knowledge to come. The man was gone, had vanished, but on the ground lay a ball of dung that had been the last thing to get a really good look at him.

The Gypsy woman took the dungball back to her wagon and baked it at low temperature in her little Gypsy wagon oven until it was dry and hard. Then she filled the cavity that the man's face had made with plaster of Paris. When this dried, she crumbled away the dung mold and there, before her, the face of her love's assassin stared back.

The impression had come out well. Pure white, much like a death mask of a famous person (one thinks, for some reason, of Voltaire) except that the assassin had made a kind of squinched *"Pew!"* face when he hit the dung, and so the mask lacked the stillness and tranquility we like to associate with the repose of death.

The Gypsy woman put the mask in her little woven bag and descended the creaky wooden steps of her wagon. She had no doubt she would find the assassin drunk and wasting his ill-gotten pesos in one of the local brothels. This was how it always was. She would find him. The white plaster cast was as good as a mug shot. She set out on his trail.

*

The Gypsy woman found the assassin drunk at a table in La Casa Pepe, surrounded by a host of fifteen-year-old whores with solid gold incisors. The assassin had just given a young boy two pesos, and in each hand the assassin held an electrode that was attached to a black box strapped around the boy's neck. (This is a Latin barroom diversion not much practiced north of the border.) The boy flipped the switch just as the Gypsy woman wove into view. The slight jolt of electricity shuddered through the assassin's body and when he saw her coming toward him, it was as if the doors of perception had momentarily blown wide open.

The Gypsy woman sat down beside him and shooed away the whores with the gold teeth. She peeked into her little woven bag and saw that the plaster mask matched the assassin's stunned mug. Just the expression was a little off.

"You are drunk," she told the assassin. "Come back to my wagon with me and have some Gypsy twat. I can tell you've never had any before—otherwise you wouldn't be here, drunk in a whorehouse."

*

Now Gypsy vulva is something else. (Go ask the Wolfman.) Drained, the assassin ended up with his tell-tale face between the Gypsy woman's sleek thighs. Not only could he smell the sweet death-smell of the sea there, but he could hear its sweet death-whisper as well, since a Gypsy woman's entrance is as convoluted and acoustic as a conch, though of course what the assassin was really hearing were the dying gasps of millions of booze-sodden brain cells giving up their infinitesimal mitochondrial ghosts.

But if you're not really all that sleepy, there's not much to do after Gypsy sex. You have a smoke. You pour yourself a drink. Since there are no tv sets in Gypsy wagons, you can do one of two time-honored things:

One) If you are the Silent Type, you can lie there in the heat with your cigarette and glass of mezcal and stare at the grease stains on the wall that start to look more and more like the silhouette of Gary Cooper.

Or

Two) If you are Garrulous, you can talk. About anything. About yourself. Love. Death.

The assassin stared at the grease stains on the wall. The Gypsy woman, tonight, was Garrulous.

"Do you believe in After Death?" she asked the assassin.

He shrugged his shoulders.

"I do not believe in it," she said. "Do you want to know why?"

The assassin shrugged his shoulders again. He was not being rude. He just wasn't finished picking the curly Gypsy hairs out of his teeth.

"I think about mummies a lot," the Gypsy woman said. "I think if there are mummies in nature, then there is no soul and life is all there is. And there are mummies in nature. Not prepared ones, like Egyptian mummies." She enunciated the *gyp* with visible distaste. "I mean natural ones. I saw some when we swung through Guanajuato.

"There are about ninety of them all together. All lined up in glass cases along one wall of a long hallway. It used to be that there were no glass cases, but the local boys kept sneaking in and breaking off the members of the man mummies. A mummified manroot"—and here she gave the assassin's a tweak—"looks sort of like a stale tobacco leaf crushed in a wagon wheel rut. It was said that the boys sold them to Asian tourists as aphrodisiacs, I don't know. Some people look for such exotica.

"Likewise the laps of the woman mummies are nothing but a sparse patch of stiff gray hairs. Some of them seem to have drifted laterally in the drying process so that they appear in the position of a holster on the woman mummy's hip. The woman mummy's breasts have fallen flat and are all dried up too. You're lucky you'll never get to see that," the Gypsy woman said ominously, but the assassin took no notice. He was busy pouring himself another glass of mezcal.

"It is not their sexual parts, but their mouths that are so arresting, for they were buried in just the attitudes they died in. Maybe the priest or local *médico* closed the eyelids of the corpses, but they did nothing about the mouth or the rest of the body. Heads thrown back and to one side, each mouth is open in a long, slanted oval, a capital "o" in italics: *O*." The Gypsy woman opened her mouth wide and jerked her jaw to one side. Her dentition was unusual and the assassin squirmed a little when he thought about the fellation he had been on the getting end of only half an hour before.

"Some of them look like they belong in a choir, but on most it is death that is evident. The most shocking is a young mother who died with her newborn during a primitive Caesarian section. There's a gaping hole where her belly was. Right *here*"—and she patted the assassin on his naked tummy just below the navel—"*you know the spot*. Whoever stood her up in the glass case had wired the infant mummy to the mother mummy's right hand. The mother mummy's right arm is extended down and slightly forward, elbow bent a little, palm out, as if the mother mummy were hefting a bowling ball. It may be that the infant mummy is staring down a bowling alley at ten white pins that look like teeth, but the infant mummy's face is *squinched*"—and the Gypsy woman enunciated this word with ominous precision—"tight like a sphincter, inscrutable. The feeling that there is Life After Death does not come to me.

"The cemetery at Guanajuato itself is walled in like a fortress, or prison. It is underneath one of these walls that the long hallway of these mummies is located. And it is because of these walls that the mummies were discovered. There is never any room left for the newly dead. It is like an eternal traffic jam. Like Mexico City. After a decade or so a body's bones are dug up and carted off to a charnel house to be burned, except for the bodies that are mummified. These are taken down into the long hallway and stood up in the glass cases.

"To be sure, their guts are gone, long ago turned to powder. But the skin remains, brittle yet leathery, like *papier mache* beef jerky. No one knows how or why. The dry climate. The composition of the soil. Dumb luck. No one knows.

"But, whatever," the Gypsy woman said, "after seeing this I cannot believe there are such things as souls. It just wouldn't make sense."

"Have another glass of mezcal," said the assassin.

*

Now the assassin was not being callous when he told the Gypsy woman to have another glass of mezcal. After all, being an assassin was just a job and had nothing to do with his real feelings about people. In fact, he was filled with a profound sense of alcohol-induced pity for her, and he wanted the Gypsy woman to believe in the reality of the human soul. Also, deep down, he didn't want her getting any ideas about another head job. He had gotten an awfully good look at those choppers. And so he suggested more mezcal.

"Picture," said the assassin, "picture a man so tiny that he has to use all his might just to pick up an ant's thigh bone.

"Picture his tiny knuckles going white because he has to squeeze so hard just to hold the ant's thigh bone over his head as he begins to swing it in a circle.

"Picture, if you can, a solitary brown hair on one of these white knuckles. Picture a lumberjack so small that he is about to swing his ax into the side of that brown hair that so towers above him.

"Picture the lumberjack's rolled up sleeves and his bulging muscles. Picture the millions of fibers that go into making up just one of these muscles.

"Now imagine a single one of these fibers stretched from the Earth to the Moon. Say, from downtown Oaxaca to the dark center of a Moon crater.

"Imagine, if you will, hordes of infinitesimal ghostly creatures creeping along this single strand like rats along the mooring rope of a docked ship.

"Imagine, furthermore, that these impossibly tiny creatures are the souls of the newly dead on their way to the Moon, where they are to take up residence for eternity in glorious empires tinier than a speck of Moon dust.

"Now," said the assassin. "Imagine a drunk asleep in a back alley. Beside him is an open bottle of mezcal. Attached to the surface of the mezcal is a fine thread that runs up through the mouth of the bottle and seems to vanish in the night sky.

"Imagine all the souls of the dead, and there are millions of new ones every night, swarming over the lip of the bottle and dropping into the mezcal. Picture them swimming with their last soulbreaths toward the slender thread that just touches the shimmery surface of the liquid.

"Well, now," explained the assassin, "the Ancients believed that there was only one of these fibers—they called it Super String Theory, I believe, but that's a little above my paygrade—and once that snapped all the dead souls were marooned on Earth and doomed to walk it eternally. In fact, however, this is not so. Every time a bottle of mezcal, or tequila, or gringo whiskey, or any other alcoholic beverage, even including some brands of anti-freeze—every time a bottle is opened up a fine thread shoots out like harpoon trailing its casting rope and *Claro!* the Earth and the Moon are connected. Myriad dead souls, like ants on honey, converge on the spot. You saw the kids in the audience after I blew the guts out of that narcissistic asshole on the trapeze."

The Gypsy woman winced.

"That's why," the assassin announced, "alcoholic beverages have such an intoxicating effect when you drink them. You feel all light and airy. It is because you are ingesting millions of dead people's souls. That's why, in fact, such beverages are called *spiritous* liquors, or sometimes simply *spirits*."

The assassin rested his case with the contented finality of a defense attorney who is certain that the jury has sucked the heady juices out of every lie he has served them up.

"But," cried the Gypsy woman, "if I drink this mezcal and experience such lightness and airiness, doesn't that stop the souls from getting to their glorious empires on the Moon?"

The assassin hadn't thought about that. He was just trying to demonstrate the existence of souls and to keep her mind occupied for a while. His thoughts fumbled for a moment, but sometimes you just can't come up with the right ending for a story. And after all, he had been drinking.

*

Henry Miller warned us somewhere that it is the utmost foolishness for a man to speak to a woman about his soul, about any souls. I don't remember his reasons exactly, but they must have been good ones because when they found the assassin's remains all that was left was a piece of his nose.

The Gypsy woman told the police that the circus hyenas had done it, but when they examined the piece of nose that was all that was left of the assassin, they discovered that the hyenas had left teeth marks that matched those the Gypsy woman had imprinted on the corner of a leftover grilled cheese sandwich that was moldering in her Gypsy wagon icebox.

"Yes. I have been in communication with the hyenas for several years. They told me I could become one of them if I went out and ate me a dead body," the Gypsy woman

193

said to Inspector Urrutia. "The assassin was already dead when I found him in La Casa Pepe," she lied. "Electrocuted. I didn't kill him."

"Are you a hyena now?" he asked her.

"Yes," she said.

Inspector Urrutia told the Gypsy woman that she would have to prove it. Hyenas had fascinated him ever since childhood—all able detectives have weird, esoteric hobbies—when he read they were worshipped as gods by awestruck bushman witch-doctors for their ability to shit white shit. This was due, he later learned from a scientific journal, to the fact that the happy family Hyaenidae dines almost solely on cadavers, calcium bones and all. He asked the Gypsy woman if she could shit white shit. If so, he was sure she could get off, even of the charges of cannibalism, since it was the nature of hyenas to chow down on dead humans.

*

Now there may be any number of things you could do in a situation like this, but the best of them would be to shit pure snow white shit.

"Not a lot," thought the gypsy woman in her cell, staring into the toilet. "Just a little . . "

The day in court came and the Gypsy woman moved stiffly to her chair. She had a family-size tube of Gleem shoved up her bum and she was praying the judge wouldn't notice the red and green flakes that characterize the imported version of the product. Her attorney winked at her but that didn't help. She still had to worry about unscrewing the cap off the tube without the judge noticing. And then the squeeze, the gut-tearing squeeze. They had practiced it all week and her attorney—who had listened with muted awe to the Gypsy woman's account from the rifle shot and obscene trapeze through to the bloody, bone-crunching climax—assured her the transparent commode he had designed would do the trick. Still she wasn't so sure. She wanted to pray but all she could think of was *Hail Mierda Full of Mierda* and that didn't sound right.

The trial commenced. The piece of nose was admitted as belonging to the assassin. The Gypsy woman's attorney made his move to establish the validity of his client's claim that she was a hyena. The transparent commode was wheeled in and placed in front of the bench, and the judge leaned forward to examine it.

While the courtroom's attention was thus distracted, the Gypsy woman removed the cap from between her buttocks by pretending that she was picking at a dingleberry.

Then she walked over to the commode, lifted her skirt about her hips, and sat down. (Her attorney had instructed her that this was called "mounting her defense.") The judge stepped down from the bench and peered through the glass where a thin worm of white paste was issuing from the Gypsy woman's rear end. He commanded her stand up and bend over and spread her cheeks, which she did. The judge pushed his nose up her behind and seemed to sniff around. Then he removed his squinched face from her posterior and closed his eyes, as if in thought. There was a smear of sweet white toothpaste on his black moustache and he licked at it, genuinely puzzled.

"*Madre de Dios!*" he finally exclaimed. "This woman is not a hyena! No filthy carcass-sucking scavenger could produce stool like this. She is an Angel sent from Heaven! Death ruled *ex visitatione Dei*. Set her free!"

And so it was entered in the books.

NOTA BENE: Contrary to the myriad insinuations in the gossip columns of the newspapers of the day, the thick envelope which the attorney of our heroine surreptitiously slipped the judge during the above proceedings contained NOT a stack of crisp new 1000 peso notes bearing the mug of El Presidente, but rather a simple white handkerchief soaked in alcohol with which to cleanse his moustache of the smear of toothpaste. And by the by, *ex visitatione Dei* is Latin and means By the Dispensation of God. But you knew that.

THE FRACTURED FAIRY TALE
RED

Once upon a time there was a wolf who lived deep in the woods. He liked living deep in the woods because there were no freeways and truck horns, no motels with blinking red neon signs that said Vacancy, no ugly gas station logos, just trees and ferns and quiet, guileless snakes and flowers that made no noise whatsoever. The wolf in his congenial environs practiced several forms of self-denial and spiritual abnegation: he pigged out neither on that which crept upon the earth, nor on that which ruled the air, nor on the denizens of the watery element. He breathed only twice a day: once upon waking and once upon retiring. He bathed with meticulous fidelity to the highest standards of hygiene by licking himself all over. He had a long wolf's tongue and could reach all the extremities of his body except, you know, those places that were not meant to be licked. But most of the time he spent in squint-eyed contemplation of the Void. And for this he required quiet, Quiet, and more QUIET.

Now it came to pass on a certain morning he was shaken out of his absorption in Nada by a disturbance—the snapping of a twig—in the undergrowth very nearby. Perhaps as close as twelve or fifteen miles, he estimated. Because he feared that the commotion might violate the perimeter of his tranquility–which he had established at a ten-mile radius from his lair–he set out grumpily in the direction of the annoyance. It was an all day journey, involving the careful and judicious deployment of blaze-markers along the route, for he was a poor woodsman and would otherwise not be able to find his way back. He used whatever he had at hand: the gold ring he wore in his nose, the buttons that were coming off his trousers anyway, a timely emergent fecal dropping.

At long last toward evening he was able to pinpoint the locus of the racket–for it resounded inside his head now like stage-thunder–that had so broken his concentration that morning. He strode indignantly into a patch of thorn bushes, which tore at his fur here and there, and glowered angrily down upon a naked and nubile young red-headed girl reclining comfortably in the underbrush:

"Wouldst thou tell me just where thou thinkest thou art going," grumbled the wolf.

"Wouldst I couldst, dear quadruped," replied the girl. "But verily, I do not even knoweth where the fuckst I am!"

"Now what's all this business about a Grandmother's House?" said the wolf the next morning. He and the naked and nubile young red-headed girl were still inside the patch of thorn bushes.

"Sex is nice, especially the first time, isn't it?" said the girl with innocent inconsequence. "I feel like I even talk different now!"

The wolf only growled. He didn't want to think about what had happened the previous night. He wished he had not so thoughtlessly dispossessed himself of his trouser buttons the day before. It had made it too easy for her.

"How do you feel, dear Wolfe?" She had added the "e" to his name because she thought it made him seem more respectable. "I mean how do you feel inside? Do you understand what I mean by *inside*? I mean really INSIDE!"

Jesus Christ, thought the wolf, I have to get rid of this Space Cadet. But he also felt obligated in a way.

"I feel like I even *think* differently," said the girl. "How do you feel like *you* think, dear Wolfe?"

The wolf took the tips of his pointed ears in his paws and pulled them down, shutting his ears tight. He grimaced and stared squint-eyed into the undergrowth. The girl talked on and on. He tried to remember his Mantra: Was it "Romulus" or was it "Lon Chaney"? He wanted to yawn, but he had already taken his morning breath. He wanted to howl at the moon, but it was mid-morning, and besides, that would have meant backsliding on certain of his vows.

"Dear Wolfe," said the girl, lifting him by the head so that he was sort of dancing on his hind legs. "Do you remember what you promised last night? Do you remember you promised me you would accompany me to Grandmother's House and chew her out but good?"

The wolf vaguely recalled something to that effect. But the night before had been a blur, like standing to the side as a freight train roared past.

"Ouch!" said the wolf, for his toes were no longer touching the ground.

The girl lifted him higher, until their noses met—for he was a small wolf, more like a dog, if the truth be known.

"You remember, doncha, Pooch!" the naked and nubile young red-headed girl hissed into his muzzle.

He nodded. Off to Grandmother's House, he thought. And then split, man.

And so off they went, the wolf trotting a few paces behind her, his eyes fixed on the cleft of her buttocks, which was open and inviting like a pie with only the thinnest of slices removed. He stopped in his tracks—where else—and slammed his head up against the trunk of a tree three times and tried to remember his Mantra again. Was it "Thomas" or was it "Virginia" or was it "N.C. State"?

"C'mon, Lassie," demanded the girl, and she shook her head in mock despair.

By and by they arrived at a typical Grandmother's House, with bone china walls and a dogskin roof.

"She's inside there," whispered the girl. "Now you go in and give her Hell and scare the shit out of her. The damned hag, she won't let me do nothin'."

The wolf whimpered and tried to back away, but the girl held him fast by the scruff. (Was it "B.O." or was it "Steppen"?)

"You promised!" said the girl. "Now go!"

The wolf trotted toward the house. (Was it something really short, like "-gang" or "-bane"? Was it "-man Jack"?) He put his forepaws on the window ledge and pressed his cold nose against the glass. Grandmother sat at a table playing cards with a Woodcutter. The Woodcutter's axe stood in a corner. He hadn't counted on a Woodcutter, let alone an axe. He was about to bolt when he heard the naked and nubile young red-headed girl behind him announce in a sort of public whisper:

"I pledgeth thee my body forever. This eve. This eve, dear Wolfe . . . "

The wolf felt his own body slip unexpectedly into gear. He pushed open the front door of Grandmother's House and stood on the threshold. His ascetic's body cast a long, scrawny shadow across the floor. Perhaps, he considered, I overdid this meatless diet business.

"Grandmother!" he announced. "Your naked and nubile young red-headed granddaughter demands—"

The four eyes at the table grew big as saucers: "A WOLF!"

The Woodcutter went for his axe. Grandmother made a dash for the cupboard, where she had stashed a cleaver.

"Get him, Hubert," cried out Grandmother. "He's skinny as a rail but the loins'll grill up fine! Now, Hubert, don't go messin' up that there new th'ow rug."

The Woodcutter's axe-blade glinted in the waning afternoon sun.

And then something strange and wonderful happened:

The wolf gobbled up the Woodcutter and polished off Grandmother for dessert. He went upstairs and put on Grandmother's black negligee and her white flannel nightcap and climbed into Grandmother's four-poster. He belched. "Wolf," he thought. That was it. That was his goddam Mantra! Just plain Wolf. No "e" on the end. How could he have forgotten? Just plain goddam *wolf*. He settled back into Grandmother's pillow and waited. For the first time in years he felt the saliva gather in his mouth like a forgotten promise.

"Dear Wolfe" came the sweet voice from the bottom of the stairs.

"O dear Wolfe" and he heard the first step creak softly.

THE TIME TRAVEL STORY
AN IMMODEST PROPOSAL

It was a long trip back there. The Time Warp was, well, warped and my back ached by the time I finally made it through. No easy journey for a gentleman of my girth. But here I was. Dublin. 1730. The year after he had published that infamous essay. We'd read it in college and it had been a welcome respite from the obscurities of Pope's *Dunciad* and the drudgery of Dr. Johnson's judgmental-isms.

I found him in his rectory. He was talking up a young lady who was clearly infatuated with his brilliance. His teeth were in such bad shape that it was understandable where all his rage and vitriol came from. But the young woman saw past this oral devastation and into the resourcefulness of his instincts and intellect. Bless her!

Sir, I said. I knew everybody said "Sir" when addressing a literary figure back in those days. Whether you were going to viciously stick him with a rapier or just bring him his tea. I liked that. It simplified things.

Sir, I said. I'm here about the secret recipes.

The young woman stood up. I wondered if she was just some chippy off the street but she looked too finely accoutered for that.

A toothsome lass, I said. You like them tender.

Laetitia, he said, ignoring the insinuation. The little locked casket.

The young gal disappeared. Dutifully. I envied his dispatch of her. They can be hard to get rid of sometimes, if you know what I mean.

He fumbled at a snuff box. Snorted once. Twice. His eyes rheumed. Ahhh.

You wanted, he said, the fricassee?

For starters, I said. You also mentioned—

So how are things in the 21st Century? Business good? The culinary arts up to snuff?

I pondered the triteness of the idiom. Up to snuff? *This* was Jonathan Swift? *The* Jonathan Swift? Inventor of Lilliput and Brobdingnag and the Struldbrugs and the Yahoos and the wise-ass talking horses whose name I could never pronounce—much less spell?

We're doing tolerably well, I said. But running a tad short of new ideas. These chic upstart gourmet restaurants are eating into our profits with their trendy fare. We've read your Modest Proposal essay again. We found it mouth-watering. And heard about the recipes. We think you were on to something.

The recipes, yes. I came up with them as a lark. An inside joke. Circulated the choicest ones among a few friends. With a note: "*Onlie* for those useless Children of the Irish Peasantry. Get them off their Parents' Backs. And into their Bellies." We wits do that sort of thing. Anything for a cheap laugh. Then they leaked out. Someone's maidservant or footman, I don't know. I almost hanged for it. The history books don't mention that. Thank God I still have a few friends in high places. Now there *were* rumors Sir Toby and Lady Millicent took things a little too far at dinner one evening with friends. A little too literally. Ugh! But *I* had no intention—

Of course, I agreed. You lacked the proper Spirit of Entrepreneurship. But today your essay has been read by millions. There are whole swathes of hungry, impecunious peoples ripe for your solution. And not a few of the better classes, truth be told.

I see. But what's in it for me? Why should I share my closest secrets with you or anyone else?

Money. Loads of it. More moolah than you can imagine. Gold, sir. Gold.

But I'm an old man now. One foot in the grave. And the other in the dunghill of my execrations. And I have my sinecure. What need do I have for untold riches?

Okay. Sure. We've worked that out too. So how's this? If not riches, then—FAME! Fame beyond your wildest imaginings! Fame beyond all measure!

Fame? I'm already famous. I'm told I am read in English Literature Departments all around the world. Even outside of them sometimes too.

Sir, I said, and I felt bad about this. Indeed you are still read. But you have been Deconstructed. You are now understood as a reactionary messenger of the most vile impulses of a privileged class with nothing but contempt for the peons you pretended to minister to. Your flock! Ha! To say nothing of your heartless seduction of that slick demure subaltern wench Laetitia and brazen reduction of her to a defecation machine!

That was *Celia*. Not Laetitia. "But—*Celia, Celia, Celia* shits!" A fine poem that. "The Lady's Dressing Room." But not *my* Letty.

Laetitia, he called, and I waited in anticipation. Letty, the casket of recipes!

We heard the rustle of copious garments from another room. A grunting sound. No flush though. (Remember: 1730) The good Dean of St. Patrick's Cathedral winced.

The chops at dinner, he complained. Did not agree with her. But a charming little groan, no?

Finally Laetitia pranced gaily in with the goods. She looked relieved. He unlocked the casket and I studied the handwritten sheets. Lousy spelling and inconsistent, clumsy capitalization and goofy italics, but they were all there. I recalled my first encounter back in my starving college days with the insight that "a young healthy Child well Nursed is at a year Old, a most delicious, nourishing, and wholesome Food, whether *Stewed, Roasted, Baked,* or *Boyled,* and I make no doubt that it will equally serve in a *Fricasie,* or *Ragoust.*" *No doubt,* he had said. Perfect. Everything was in order.

Fame, he muttered. "That last infirmity of a noble mind."

I recalled my English major Milton. Nothing memorable to eat in that whole damn epic poem of his but a poisonous apple. Not that I read it cover to cover, of course.

But it was time to warp back to the Present. Wrap things up. I had the recipes. Mission accomplished. I made to take my leave. To skedaddle. Split. Take a powder. Be gone. Before the geezer changed his mind!

But he was not quite finished.

This new restaurant chain you mentioned in your exploratory timeslung missive, he grumbled with more than a hint of suspicion—perhaps he doubted my guarantee of a New and Enduring Fame. What do you plan to call it?

That's easy, Sir, I said. *Jonathan Swift's*—we'll stick with the original Irish theme—*McBABIES!*

THE EPISTOLARY STORY
PENPALS

Back of Y.M.C.A. Building
Davao City, Philippines
Nov. 24, 1990

Dear Mr. Harold Nitcombe Ill,

Hello! probably you'll be surprised w/ this letter of mine and I would like to tell you that my friend is a bona-fide member of Pot O' Golden Honey International Penpal Club, Inc and she passed your name onto me and I'm very glad of it coz I like to correspond a foregn man like you there.

Perhaps you wish to know my name & my self. Well, let me introduce my self, I'm Luz Lloren, 23 yrs old Filipina, brown complection, black hairs and eyes, 5' 3" in height, 110 lbs—little bit slim, still studying in Southeastern Mindanao Teachers College, Davao City, Philippines, taking up of Bachelor of Elem Ed 4th year, descent, a devouted catholic & religious, kind, loving, understanding, sinple mind, conservative, hospitiable, friendly, fun-be-with, thoughtful, diligent, frank, & one-man-woman. And before I forget I'm still single.

Well! if there are questions personal you may want to ask me, you may & be open-minded and I don't have ANY HANG UPS on that regards.

Please know I was chosen your name from a 70 list of names coz you are a teacher and have beautiful name and of age to be settle down & stable & not chase.

Harold, I didn't expected that I can received your name, so I just find a time to write for you believing that you won't fail to answer me. I appreciate your letter knowing you in details.

Your new Penfriend (?)

Luz Lloren

PS Enclose herewith is my photo. I apologize I am not the beauty but am sunny.

*

Gus's Hotel
East 12th and Ironbridge
Cleveland, Ohio, U.S.A.
Dec. 29, 1990

Dear Luz Lloren,

Thank you very much for the sweet and gentle letter of self-introduction which arrived only the other day. Naturally I am overjoyed at the prospect of becoming your penpal. When I sent in my name and personal check to Pot O' Golden Honey Girls International, Inc. I hardly expected to be contacted so soon by such a charming and bright creature as yourself. The Pot O' Golden Honey people sent me a copy of their Spring issue of *Honey Pots*, which included photos and biodata of some 200 odd young Asian women, and I selected 25 of them for possible penpal relationships. But so far none of them have responded to my feelers. So it is with greatest pleasure and anticipation that I write to you now. It was a lot of typing, as my Word Processor is in hock.

Let me tell you a few things about myself first, and then I'll ask you some questions about yourself and your life these days. I am 42 years old, a lifelong bachelor, 5' 7" in height, a little overweight at 207 lbs. (but dieting), an ardent Pacifist, very conservative in my views concerning sexual immorality, open-minded otherwise, possessive of a sense of humor, deeply concerned about the present World Crises, free-spirited and anguished. Also, I am immune to cancer. I am a college graduate (East Youngstown State Teachers College) and am presently on temporary leave-of-absence from my position as a teacher of Computer Business Arts for the Cleveland (Ohio) Public School System. This leave-of-absence was granted at the request of certain influential people who feel, and I think rightly so, that my special abilities ought to be given the opportunity to germinate and flower while I calm down and get some rest. But more about that later, when you get to know me better.

Right now I want to give you especial thanks for the photograph you enclosed. I truly wonder at the creamy brownness of your skin. For an hour a day this week I have been staring at you and shaking all over, which is how I enter your image in Deep Mind. Deep Mind is forever, but I can access it only during states of extreme agitation and anguish while lying on my back on the bathroom floor with the door closed. Don't worry—you cannot be harmed by it. Like hypnosis, you cannot be compelled to do anything in Deep Mind against your will. Until I get to know you more, I'll leave it at that.

Finally I would like to know about your everyday life, your hometown, family, the latest news in your country concerning domestic political affairs, radar surveillance, the Communist insurgency, any recent and/or unusual seismologists' reports, birth control methods, and whether or not there is any truth to the story that a UFO landing pad was found atop Malacanang Palace the day it was stormed, lost Japanese gold hordes, etc.

Deepest regards,

Harold Nitcombe III.

PS I am enclosing a recent photo taken at my residence—the bright splash of light obscuring the top of my face is the reflection of the flash in my mirror. I will try to do better next time.

*

Back of Y.M.C.A. Bldg.
Davao City, Philippines
Jan. 21, 1991

Dear Harold,

Hi! Good day to you! I was so very glad to received your letter w/ch was very interesting & informative. Thanks, also for your handsome picture but that I can't see your face cleanly because of over flashlight. I'm very sorry if I had answer you too late coz I'm waiting of my allowance and I'm little short for stamps but alright now. Student have lot of expenses in Philippines is still very poor any more. You know?

Though I read your letter several times if I'm not busy w/ my studies. But please be patient w/ my learning. I almost can't understand your writing coz you know my English is not full. So some times I have to guess your meaning even though the word is foregn to me. Oh! Before I forgot—Probably you can't know to pronounciate my name in the Philippines. It is said like this: Looz Il-yor-en. Most of our names were in Spanish origin since Phil. was under a colony of Spain for 350 yrs. or 3 centuries & half.

I will try answer your questions about my self, family, & etc. Like I said in first introduction letter, I am college student 4th year. My life in Philippines is I'm just contented w/ what I am now, but I still have to aspire to finish my course as my number Ace priority. My mother lives in a small village in Bitauen province but my father is not home. I have the older sister (Vera) lives here in Davao City and working at library here at my SEMTCO (Southeastern Mindanao Teachers College). She is a older but not married sister. Another sister (Purisima) is married teacher in Cagayan de Oro. One brother married also. He works on the ~~boast~~ boats.

To answer your questions:

In politics affairs we are always waiting for kudeta from Army or Air Force but Mrs. Acquino is somewhat strong yet. We like her but have no jobs in big companies since aren't any big companies nowdays. Don't worry the Communists (NPA) insurgent because they are cowardice and just insecured. They simply looking their place on the sun but actually they're losing the war. Do not believe on their propaganda.

With regards to Artificial methods of Birth Control. Where 80% of the population here in Phil. is catholic the church doctrine about this matter do not allow the practice of Artificial methods control, except for a rhythym method. Vesectomy, pills, IUD are prohibited by the church but then there are some artist and society woman can practice birth control on Artificial way. Even my sister in law is being ligated. I hear some times a lover wants the woman en culo but you can not but love him to say yes. I am sorry to say.

I can't say about seismologists reports coz I don't know. Who are they? Can you tell me?

But only one newspaper said that about UFO landing place at Malacanang. How can you know about this too? I think you are very wise as a person.

The Japanese gold hordes is coming into the Phil. now. They like Filipina ladies and sing at new karaoke houses everywhere in Manila it is said. (I never been Manila.)

Please, Harold, at your age now, are you already engaged to some beautiful woman here in Ohio?

Thank you for putting my picture in your Deep Mind. It is such a lovely your thought of me. May I lie down there on Valentine heart pillows? You Know, Valentines day is coming next month. Can you tell me about Valentines day in the USA? I will tell you about that in the Phil. in my next letter maybe.

Lastly I would like to bade you Goodbye.

Warmest regards,

Luz

PS Here is another photo for you in "Deep Mind". But I can't send many because of the money cost. L. Ll.

*

Gus's Hotel
East 12th and Ironbridge
Cleveland, Ohio, U.S.A.
Feb. 13, 1991

Dear Luz,

Thanks for your wonderful and informative letter. First, let me reassure you that I am not engaged to "some beautiful woman here in Ohio." Certainly I have had a number of female friends in my life, including a couple of Registered Nurses (psychiatric) and others, nevertheless I am free of all attachments, save in Deep Mind now that I have entered you there. Forever, I hope.

As to the seismologists' reports. A seismologist is a

highly trained scientist who monitors tremors in the earth's crust by means of a seismograph (seismos=shock, quake), which can predict and measure earthquakes, volcanic activity, slipping plates, etc. These instruments register only the grossest data, however. In fact, there are oscillations of the earth's surface that are too subtle and fine for them, but which sometimes clearly come near to knocking me off my feet. The reason why I have to lay down on my back on the bathroom floor for long periods of time. The bathroom is the safest place in my home (Gus's Hotel, East 12th and Ironbridge) because the bathroom window has been boarded up and hence flying glass no danger. Last week I tried to contact you telepathetically through Deep Mind holding your photo before my face, but I believe Mrs. Imelda Marcos' leftover bastard daughters—she has a brood of two thousand two hundred and twenty two of them which can fly but only after leaving their bottom halves on the ground while the top halves ascend upward as Air Guardian Vampires into the Noo-sphere where their deviltry can knock down messages sent by me and other penpals to Filipina girls—blocked my head pulses. This explains the presence of those two thousand two hundred and twenty two pairs of shoes in the basement of Malacanang Palace which the newspapers naively explain away as simple vanity and greed. If you happen to find the bottom half of one of these beings standing up in the middle of the night, you should pour one half pound of salt on it. It will shrivel up and vaporize and when the bastard female Air Guardian Vampire returns to its bottom half and finds nothing there it will halve (ha ha) to keep flying around until exhausted at daylight it falls to the ground and is run over by buses. Can you verify this for me? I learned about this in a story in *Vampires Tonite* given to me by a fleeting, improvised simulacrum named Count Besmirchneck who appeared that evening sitting on my stomach (I was lying down on the bathroom floor, remember) while I was trying to contact you telepathetically by staring at your photo and shaking all over. He said his name means something very dirty in a foreign language, but he wouldn't repeat it. Also, I think he has a bespoke tailor. Then he fell dead face forward into a plate of beef stew he had brought with him. It was exactly like the Mekong Delta starting all over again. Then he left.

Before he fell dead face forward into the plate of beef stew, however, Count Besmirchneck instructed me that I will not be able to contact you through Deep Mind using the two photos you have given me. He said the minimum I would need would have to be a photograph of you in a yellow bikini. Yellow is important because it is the color of gold, my sister's soul, and Cory Aquino, and can open up links between Deep Mind and satellites for transmission. Bikini because anybody can wear clothing whereas Deep Mind can find you better on Search Mode (there are six billion people on this planet, not counting fleeting, improvised simulacrums) if it knows what you look like more. I hate like hell to bring this up so early in our friendship, being shy, and am only relaying to you what Count Besmirchneck indicated. He said nothing about any particular pose so you are pretty much free to do it in your own way, I think.

When I was in the third grade each student in my class was given a packet of 25 Valentine's Day cards and we had to sign each one and give one to every member of the class, regardless. This was an important lesson in Universal Love which I have not forgotten. Of course, no one understood at that time the meaning of the red heart pierced by an arrow. The word "heart" derives from the word "hurt" and the heart shape itself is a design of the pubic deltoid (the pointy part) and a pair of buttocks (or breasts). That is, love is anguish. I don't understand the Baby Cupid business so well except that maybe it means pregnancy. I was very interested in what you said about birth control because I don't believe in contraception. I had to arrange an abortion for a woman many years ago, and I have cause to believe my troubles began around that time.

I am going to sign off now. But I am enclosing a counter check for $50 to help you cover the photograph expense, postage stamps, and also for some bags of salt (would fifty pounds be enough?—I don't know). You know, it is hard to believe we have never met—I feel I can say my deepest thoughts to you without fear of disapproval. This is a rare thing.

Deepest regards,
Harold

*

Behind Y.M.C.A. Building
Davao City, Philippines
March 4, 1991

Everdearest Harold,

<u>Kumusta</u>? Do you know what it means? It means in Tagalog (Phil. language) How are you? I hope you are in the best of everything. As I am upon receiving your letter number #2.

Thank you for explaining me the American Valentine Day idea. (And also for the enclosed V.D. card. It made me feel imported.) I didn't know had such a big meaning to you. Also red heart. I didn't know either that you had anguish about it. Was your heartbroken in the past days that you say your sorrow to me? If she did this she was FOOL coz you are good man and wisdom. Then let me say about Valentine Day here in Phil. is very popular too as well. Some student organizations even take advantage of fund raising by selling ropes to be sent to their sweat hearts. Disco houses are filled w/ disco gores usually sweat hearts—during Feb. 14 night that is how they celebrate Valentine Day. If we have no Valentine partner we titled ourself for "Firing Squad" & we just laugh and stand up at a wall and watch the partners. Others will just say, my Valentine partner is Dr. Jose "Noli Me Tangere" Rizal our national hero whose monument is in our public park in every city because he is alone in parks w/ no partner. Also he was shotted by firing squad when he died because of Independence Movement. But of course we don't get shotted like that but maybe a arrow through a heart—like you say!

Harold, who cook your own food & who will shop the grocery for you? Who cleans your rooms & doing laundry for you? Do you have a maid? If I'm just around w/ you I'll have to pay my services for you in exchange for the money you sent me. Your money was really a great help to me.

But I am trouble what you say concerning Air Guardian Vampires are leftover bastrad brood of Mrs. I. Marcos. It is true in Phil. some people will say that vampire ladies leave a bottom half of them on a ground of earth to fly up and away to frolic. But also I think this can be lied too. Why? I can tell you. My friend Flormina was attack one night by the men who have not a job. Of course they rape of her coz they were many and she was one. When she did try tell police of this, the men said she was vampire girl, leave her bottom half standing on ground of earth and they only rape just that bottom half they said. They said bottom half didn't struggle but was just the animal. Why did she go out in a night? they told the Police officer. Of course she had boyfriend was one of the raptors. So Police he agreed w/ those men to went away free of charge, all of them, coz on the bottom half she have only some bruises, not top half. I don't ever believe Flor could be vampire girl. But now if she want to go out in the night she is allways scared of it. A pity. But I know there is vampires here in Phil. Impact, I was surprise in your letter you could know these. It is fact they can leave the bottom half on the ground of earth when they flies. But I didn't know about the half pound salt. (Thank Count Besmirchneck for me. You are lucky to have the friendship him.) Or they were Air Guardian Vampires I didn't know. I thought just vampires, so we say here. So I believe you, now. But Harold! I got to say some truthful thing. Before I thought that maybe you are crazy man—maybe had a head knock up in a incident. So can't think rightly. But you are correct about Philippine Vampires and must be wise, also Count B. Still I surprise they can be Mrs. Imelda Marcos' bastrad brood. Coz 2,222 is many babies for a woman even former First Lady of my Country. Nowdays the Davao City newspaper has to say they are <u>foregn</u> vampires come our country March through November every year on some visas. Drink Filipina hemogoblin w/ch is reddest in the world (coz Special Hole in Philippine Sky let's in sunlight shine most cleanly. Said Mrs. Marcos in a newspaper story Why I Love My Philippines.)

Pertaining to the picture you've ask to me, Yes! I insert this but I'm very much sorry that there's an ink on it coz when my druggist to develop it give this to me, there are some scars on it, I think this is from medecine chemicals. Sorry that it was not in the beach coz I felt ashamed, since not all people here wearing swim suit except the artist & society girl who have freedom.

Finally I am very much thankful w/ your $50 check. I thank you so much for your thoughtfulness, how I wish people in the whole world be as thoughtful as you. Harold, I'm very much worried if I could not send you any little things, coz I'm still student & don't have yet an income of my own. I hope you will understand the life of being student because my allowance is always on budget & got even short sometimes. But let me say when I got your check I look at it and I really can believe you says of mental telephaty coz I imagining there and then to meet you and conversing w/ each other, showing smile & etc.

Dearly lovingly,

Luz

P.S. I was sorry to hear about your friend Count Besmirchneck. It can hurt to have the close friend fall dead into food at a dinner table. My father did that one time, drunk. Then we got him up again. But it was not the same as before. He was so bored. Then disappeared. Probably he ran w/ widow Mrs. Niepes because she disappeared same time at w/ch my father fall into the food at table.

*

Gus's Hotel
East 12th and Ironbridge
Cleveland, Ohio, U.S.A.
March 28, 1991

My dearest Luz,

A billion thanks for your latest letter (& enclosure). The bikini picture was a delight to behold, and it is okay that it was taken in your room and not on the beach— Modesty becomes a woman, to my mind. On the evening news tonight it was reported that airports will soon have detectors which through computer technology will have the power of x-ray vision. That is, the machine can peek through clothing and reconstruct a nude computerized image of the naked passenger on a screen, including, they implied, even stretch marks. Of course, Deep Mind has had this capability for some years now, but now the word is out. It was only a matter of time, I guess.

This brings up an interesting problem. Though you were able to pick me up on mental telepathy (watch your spelling, dear girl) by staring at the $50 check I sent, I haven't had the same success with the bikini photo. Apparently it is not specific enough. (The bikini—top and bottom—can be removed by special computer enhance-ment—originally my invention, though discretion kept me from applying for the patent—but you are standing sidewise and I can't turn you around—I don't have ho-logram capabilities, you know. That's a decade down the road.) Among other things, I have to ask you a personal question: Do you shave your armpits? Don't get me wrong—it doesn't make any difference to me (tho I'm curious yellow, as they used to say)—but Deep Mind needs the datum. Better yet, and Count Besmirchneck is backing me up on this, a nude picture might provide the breakthrough Deep Mind needs. Of course I know this is a terrible thing to ask a woman, especially a virgin, and I don't suppose there's any delicate way to put the unprecedented. But, as you know from that brief moment you stared at the check and glimpsed me across Time Zones, we are very close to cracking the problem. Search Mode of Deep Mind is only as good as the data I can input.

Most important is the clear distinction I want to draw between what I am asking you—and what is known as dirty pictures. Did you know that I can walk down to the end of my block and buy a magazine that shows naked women trussed up like Christmas turkeys, bung agape and all? I have sometimes thought of vaporizing the place with head pulses—It is a small porno shop with a floor space of less than 150 m^2 and rents, I understand, for less than \$400 a month, or so the proprietor has hinted under telepathic questioning—but there are Hispanic families on the second and third floors who would be cast out into the street if the structure one day disintegrated. And this is only a small part of my anguish. I'm sure you can understand.

Now, I want you to understand the nature of Deep Mind. Deep Mind came into existence on July 4, 1976, at Thistledown Race Track in an eastern suburb of Cleveland. Moments before Post Time for the seventh race (3:50 PM) I stared at the Tote Board and saw all the telephone numbers of all the people and their ascendants who had ever lived and died in America flash in orange lights. This was in Wagering on the seventh race. I had to go into the Men's Room and lie down on the floor on my back shaking all over because I knew I was going to raise the dead of America simulcast during the 1 minute and 13 seconds it took the field to run the six furlongs, which I did. The dead did not go immediately to Eternity but my rising them is now a guarantee that they will. This obliterates Time, or at best gives it only the status of an Illusion. The spread of Personal Computers is one consequence of my feat, as was my first ambulance ride. I was in a john stall and my feet stuck out and I have had no reason to return to Thistledown since. The race was won by a three-year-old thoroughbred filly named Flutterbutt, Javier Felix up.

That is the origin of Deep Mind. I am sorry that the dead of the Philippines were not raised on July 4, 1976, but it is my understanding that, even though the Philippines is the second-largest English speaking country in the world, according to the language of treaties Filipinos are not Americans. Also, I am sorry to hear about your father. But these things happen.

All my love,

Harold

PS I have again enclosed a counter check for $50. Buy yourself something lovely with it, and give my regards to your family. May all be well.

PPS One final question—Why do Philippine people give ropes to their sweethearts on Valentine's Day?

*

Behind of Y.M.C.A. Bldg.
Davao City, Philippines
April 19, 1991

Everdearest Harold,
Hello! my dear, good day to you, hope everything is fine, for me the same as usual but still thinking of you & looking your picture & trying to make the mental telepathies w/ you again.

You know, the day your letter arrive I knew before it was came coz a wall lizard scurry behind a mirror while

I am at studying. So I knock three times on wood of my desk to mean a friend arrive or a letter friend if a lizard does so. It is superstitional I know, but your letter come any way that day. So I give house lizard some big bug foods and he EATS! More good lucks! Old people's have such kind ideas here in Phil. like that. I tell you some more some day next letters after ask my mother them.

A million thanks for the check again. You are God-sended. Maybe if you ask how I use it, I just buy my new blouse (school color), shoes (black) and P200 for my tuition this month, P65 umbrella (monsoon) & others & now have only P50 for my riding of motor tricycle back and forth daily. My allowance hasn't arrived yet from my mother who is a poor farmer w/o the husband more so thanks a lot w/ your money. I felt ashamed already to always received your money w/o any rendering service being gratitude or thankfulness of your money.

But Dear Harold, I have some question. What is Deep Mind that you can rose the Dead of America in a race track on July 4, 1976? I am a catholic girl & religious and it hurt me to think you to done all this alone in Mens Room floor of such rich people place. Maybe you could been injuried. I don't understand What is Thistledown race track in suburb Cleveland, America? You know it is April this month here in Phil. and we had the Easter weak and the

Good Friday was the day my friend Josie her cousin decide go up the church in San Fernando Pampanga on the cross to be crucified for sins (he did bad thing in Surigao but not caught but some peoples know so he do it show pentances). But I think he did not rose any Deads, just want the change of his ways w/ doing it. Likely you don't know July 4, 1946 is Philippine Independence Day also like USA has. So maybe you also rose the Phil. Deads but not known about it. I have contraction my heart to think all this things you do. I think it is better you just work job of teacher w/o wants to be more. Man who rose the Deads will have to be responsable for all the souls got up, like Jesus Christ Our Savior. Or maybe you already had done some bad thing like Josie cousin needs pentances too. But I can't believing that you. If you have done such thing, you must tell me so I can understand about you. If you have murder to a man, I can understand, but the blood will boil out, they say. A murder, a raptor, a theif God will love and save w/ a cross. Only man the God can not love on his bosom is the betraitor, the Judes, and suicidists. So I'm telling you this. Please Harold, I can worry & fret. You must explain to me your Culture thinking way coz in Phil. we never rose the Deads by this race track way, only in prayer. I worried too much what the priets could guess if reading the letter. Maybe priets think you hermetic of apocstasy and hellbound. Later I will say the more about Fathers Priets reading the penpals letters now days (Cory Acquino) and mine too. Just please make no mistake your words don't cause the problems anti-Church. You can not be Jesus I can not be Virgen Maria.

Okay?

In your letter you ask me about the hairs of Armpits. You know I just always clean and shave those hairs because I don't like that. Same other Filipinas but not all.

Harold, I may not want disappoint you but, I'm very sorry that I could not send you the nude picture. It's against our custom & hope you will understand me. I'll be substituting for another picture okay? And I could not wear a panty & bra coz I have a monthly period (Menstruation). Maybe next time this.

Also, do you have a friends like to write a penpal coz my sister Vera would wish to correspond them. Can you recommend her? How about the Count Besmirchneck? Is his health okay except to fall in the food forward face some times? He is married or engaged or has a girlfriend already? Vera is my older sister age no problem. But I'm sorry if my question is too much so please I'm sorry.

Lastly, I give you lovingly a kiss for the good night sleep.

Love,

Luz

P.S. One more last question: On the envelope backside you put some words like these:

ELVIS LIVES,

VEILS EVILS

What does the words mean? We know the Elvis Pressly in Phil. long time ago die from some poisons. Davao City newspaper last year say he is live yet. Is the story true? Rose from Deads?

P.S.S. I am sorry. My handwriting is too bad. I didn't meant ropes in last letter. I mean roses.

*

Gus's Hotel

East 12th and Ironbridge

Cleveland, Ohio, U.S.A.

May 11, 1991

My Dearest Luz,

Halleluiah, Luz! These are heady, intoxicating evenings! You ask about the fleeting, improvised simulacrum named Count Besmirchneck who visited me first by sitting on my stomach in my bathroom and later fell dead face forward into a plate of beef stew before leaving? Well, he visited again three nights ago. And I found that I had made a terrible error. Because of his thick accent—I <u>knew</u> he was a <u>Russian</u>—I understood his name to be Count Besmirchneck but it is not Besmirchneck at all. It is Comrade Bessmirtnykh and he is Foreign Minister of the Soviet Union. This means, perforce, that I am the Secretary of State of the United States because Foreign Minister and Secretary of State mean the same thing universally. To be frank, I have long held suspicions that I am the true Secretary of State of the United States but as I had <u>never</u> received an invitation to a cabinet meeting I thought it best to keep the news of my appointment under my hat. The man whom you see in the newspaper is an acting imposter and now I have proof. Foreign Minister Bessmirtnykh has given me an invisible tablet engraved with Five Points which I must follow in order to be recognized as the Sec'y of State. They are:

Point #1: Renounce all forms of self-gratification in view of the coming merger of the United States of America with the Philippine Islands (Republic of the Philippines). This includes masturbation <u>and</u> nose-picking.

Point #2: Write letters to all of the world's leaders announcing my intention to raise the dead of their nations as I rose the dead of America on July 4, 1976. These raisings will take place on the corresponding chief national holiday of each nation so that appropriate fanfare will be available. That is, Bastille Day for France, Hitler's Birthday for Germany, etc.

Point #3: Vaporize Rusty's Emporium of Love (porn shop) on the corner of Ironbridge and East 10th after finding jobs and new, clean lodgings for the Hispanic families on the second and third floors of the building. Instruct Rusty on the nature and purpose of Universal Happiness.

Point #4: Invent something useful which will bring in enough money to carry out Point #5. Don't forget to patent it.

Point #5: Fly directly to Davao City, Mindanao, Philippines, and take in Holy Wedlock Miss Luz Lloren of said city and country after redeeming Mother's wedding ring from pawn broker (kitty-corner to Rusty's). See to it that she wears yellow.

Of course, I haven't asked you how you would feel about being the bride of the Secretary of State of the United States. But—best news of all!—Foreign Minister Bessmirtnykh has given his wholehearted approval to the match, and in fact has promised to give away the bride as your father may be dead (though he's still invited). The only thing that worries me is Bessmirtnykh's habit of falling dead face forward into his food (he did it again 3 nights ago into his chili) and leaving without saying goodbye. Perhaps it is a kind of Russian thing but it doesn't look good on the emissary of a foreign government and makes me suspicious. Can you advise me on this? I can't understand why I am being tortured and the rest of the world condones this in innuendoes. That night after Foreign Minister Bessmirtnykh left on my tv Johnny Carson whispered something to his guest and it was about me as they were looking directly at me in my chair and smiling. The guest was a Nobody Cowboy Poet. Also, as to our wedding, it will go forward provided my Mother's Spirit does not object (it's her ring technically). But don't worry. I know she will like you. She always commented on the charm and efficiency of the Filipina nurses in Shock when I was in and out of the hospital for those years of rest. But more about that another time.

And, gentlest Luz, I have been kicking myself for a month now for having had the audacity to ask you for a n*de photo. I am truly and deeply sorry. I quite fully appreciate that your culture prohibits you from posing thus. And I have the profoundest and sincerest respect for cultures that place a premium on female modesty of the pudenda. This demonstrates a high level of moral development which is no doubt under siege by expansionist, materialistic cultures like my own which have guardian airport bomb detectors that can see through clothing for weapons and now even register the private parts on a computer screen. I once applied for one of those jobs with my background but was turned down for "unspecified" reasons. Makes you think, doesn't it?

Finally, I'm afraid I cannot recommend anyone as a penpal for your sister Vera at this time. I do not think she would find Foreign Minister Bessmirtnykh a reliable correspondent, in spite of his political connections and savvy. Also, he is 6' 10" and weighs (my guess) close to 400 lbs. Sometimes he snaps at the air from side to side when he walks like a duck. Other times he walks with his chin up in the air like a horse fording a river. The bespoke zipper of his fly is three feet long and takes fifteen minutes to undo when he has to eliminate. And he does not photograph well, due to being irradiated during the Chernobyl incident. Has Vera considered sending in a smiling photo and her biodata to Pot O' Golden Honey International? I would try this first—perhaps she will fare as fortunately as you and I.

I am again enclosing a check for $50 made out to you. A bra and panties photo will be fine.

I do not know who wrote ELVIS LIVES, VEILS EVILS

on the back of my envelope. I will speak to F.M. Bessmirtnykh. (Are you okay?)

All my love,

Harold

*

Back of Y.M.C.A. Building
Davao City, Philippines
June 15, 1991

Everdearest Harold,

Sorry for that I was not able to reply you soon coz I'm
very busy at this week, making lesson plan or whatever to
be prepared in my teaching coz you know that I'm already
intern at this month and I feel so hard coz many divices
to made for my pupils. So this is time that I need money
to buy of my divices so I think that is the will of God
that my problems will solve: So I thank you very much
for being so thoughtful of sending a little amt. of money
($50) for me w/c help me very much in buying all the re-
quirments of teaching practice. I was able to buy visual
aids and so on w/c I use in my teaching intern time. I hope
there would be more people like you who knows how to
share even just a little of that he had. It's not just only that
we account but for the good deeds of a person. Harold, I

really merit you on that. And I'm even worried how I can pay you back for all the goodness, kindness, thoughtfulness you have extended me.

Congratulations to being now the Secretary of United States, but I don't understand it. Is a kind of mask face you can buy in a shop for the Festival of Holloween in America? In the Phil. we have the festival too pokes the fun at politics leaders. And they have the Las Fallas in Valencia, Spain, I read in a book about it. Make some statues in paper and water and then bonfire them every years. You and Forn. Min. Bessmirtnyhk have drink party your house all the time?

Now I had better tell you about Mrs. President Acquino very angry nowdays about too much Filipinas goes overseas to be domestics servants in Hong Kong and the Singapore for the rich people. (They has jokes saying how Filipina maid bend over to wash a floor if the Chinese wife she is out at department store the Chinese husband lifted up the Filipina dress backside and give her some praises like cry out OH! A melons field is now in blooms kissed under a round face of moon!) Also Mrs. President Acquino doesn't like mail order brides to foregn men coz of bad treatments and they sometimes become prostitutes they have falling outs w/ her husbands/family. So Filipina woman has must gets some permissions from a priets in her city marry American man or other type man (not Filipino). Priets wants to know How long you know this guy? He is truly a single man? He can support you in life? You never before met him at all but love the other? Show me the correspondents letters have to be six month time of writing back & forth, the priets will say to her. So I am keeping your letters for me for that time in future. But I sometimes will worry coz, you know I don't understand every words in them. Just a generous idea and warm nature of your habit of heart.

Now here is my picture again since I can rent a camera from my friend & buy a film & only my niece picturing me therefore when your check arrived I gave her P100 being response of her services and it includes thankfulness to her and secrecy. I hope you can keep this to your album & don't let this bra & panties picture frightened to the mouse (joke only).

Before I forget my sister would not like to publish her name in Pot 'O Golden Honey International, Inc coz she could not guarantee to answer all letters she might disappointed them. She likes introducing coz at least, you know also the person very well & and you know also already about me. Her height is 5' 3", weight 115 lbs. Age 34 yrs. Little bit slim, brown complection. I wouldn't say she's beautiful and she's attractive. She has a good body figure.

Finally I got ask one more question you. Why did you go in Hospital before? I know in America they put a Killer in there if he say at the court he carried off by insanity passion crime. You?

Again, thanks for your 50 dollar. I can't reply to you in some material things except my love for you. I LIKE YOU. I miss your words.

Love,

Luz

*

Gus's Hotel

East 12th and Ironbridge

Cleveland, Ohio, U.S.A.

July 7, 1991

Dear Luz,

Were you trying to contact me by mental telepathy 2 nights ago July 5, 1991, at exactly 19:43 PM (which would have been July 6 12:43 PM in Davao City according to Time Zones)? If so, I am sorry I could not answer back because at just that moment the data was being processed in Deep Mind Torture that my half-sister, Lydia Ottava Rima, is in reality a Negress. So I couldn't respond. As you know, when data is being processed in Deep Mind Torture I have to lie on my back on the bathroom floor with the door shut so the other residents of Gus's Hotel can't get in. Otherwise everything will come out wrong. She was the sister my mother never mentioned so which I had to separate from myself on Oct. 12, 1967 (Columbus Day) when I was a freshman in college. I separated her by ejecting a gold foil orb from between my eyes which was spherical like a Christmas tree ornament and dittered around my head in an orbit twice from right to left. Then It stopped and I saw it was her and then she blinked (the whole orb, I mean) and invaginated into thin air. Shortly thereafter she became impregnated by the President of East Youngstown State University and I never saw her again till now. Now she is a Negress and was posing full frontal nude for Deep Mind that night from a secret broadcast location, possibly Rusty's. When I glimpsed her she barked orders at me and invaginated into thin air again without a trace except for the odor of burnt electricity. But I know the child she bore the President of East Youngstown State University was only a skeleton with a pipe in its mouth and an Abraham Lincoln hat and a shawl.

Then Foreign Minister Bessmirtnykh arrived on her heels and showed me the copy of Playboy magazine in which you posed nude. I was deeply wrought up until he pointed out that you used a blonde woman's body to conceal your identity and did it only for the money. So it's okay. Then the Playboy morphed into a sausage pizza and F. M. Bessmirtnykh fell dead face forward into it and left. If you don't want him at the wedding, just let me know. The problem is he's the only credible witness I have that I am the true Secretary of State of the United States. At any rate we will have to hire security guards to keep him away from the wedding cake, which will be designed in Deep Mind by computer.

When Bessmirtnykh started to get that I'm-Going-To-Fall-Dead-Face-Forward-Into-My-Food look on his face, I commanded him to cease and decist. I told him I am just plain tired of cleaning up food that is never there when you go to wipe it up. He explained that this was a trick he had learned from your own Joker Arroyo, Philippine statesman and begetter of I. Marcos' 2,222 bastard children, Female Air Guardian Vampires. He said that this was the only possible way for him to "bow out" and get back to the Kremlin. Then he walloped the pizza with his schnozz like my words meant nothing to him.

But enough of that! Let me tell you that you contin-

ue to thrill me! The bra and panties snapshot is terrific!
Thank you! Especially the white high heels and the fact
that the thumbnail on your left hand is painted white.
This is exactly the sort of detail I can feed into Deep Mind
Search Mode to sort you out, but Deep Mind still had great
difficulty trying to remove your panties and failed. Is it
possible that your natural Modesty is capable of blocking
Deep Mind's endeavor to locate you? All it gets is a sort of
"pebbled glass" effect, a ripply shadow and no black hair
at all. Please keep in mind my suffering.

But I don't want to trouble you like this. I am enclosing
a check for $50. The lady teller at my bank who cashes
my disability checks wanted to know if I am supporting
a poor orphan overseas in South America. That's where
she thinks the Philippines is. So I showed her your photo-
graphs (I carry them with me at all times) and she became
red-faced and told me to scram. I shook on the bus all the
way home. Sometimes I see her on television commercials
spoiling dinner by using the wrong product and then getting advice from a Voice. I am surprised the bank lets her
handle all that money.

I look forward to hearing from you soon. I will do my
best to contact you through Deep Mind by mental telepathy but the Air Guardian Vampires can easily knock

down head pulses that aren't specific enough in detail. You try too.

All My Love,
Harold

*

Behind Y.M.C.A. Bldg.
Davao City, Philippines
August 7, 1991

Evermostdrearest Harold,

I was so overjoyed to received your letter w/ an enclosed check. Thanks again a lot. Every day I missed your letters w/ your very good & fluent grammar that would make me learn. I could understand English very well but not as fluent as Americans speak of it. I'm very poor in oral but not so much in writing where I can freely & fully express my idea and thoughts. Well, what can you say w/ my English? Please comment and give me your recommendation for the future life speaking English.

You know I'm so busy doing my homeworks for end of the college and especially my baby thesis must done. You know I will graduate in this October 31th and I wish all

245

my heart out you can come to be there and see. Though I know you can not, I still have the hopes. W/o your kind helps maybe I did not get completed my effort. But! Know! If you'll be coming I can take you on the beach outside city limits. I will bring you to Bilang-bilang (Open Air) w/ a number of Barbie Q. stands, so you could eat & taste Davao Barbie Q. Chicken, and I will let you eat different kinds of seafoods (fresh) crabs & shrimps (We have plenty here) & it is very cheap. I will let you eat the Kinilaw—this is uncooked fish chopped into small pieces washed by a vinegar & mixed again w/ a very fresh vinegar not in manufacturing company. Then, it is mixed w/ so many ingredients: Like pepper, ginger, onions, lemon juice, plus food seasonings. I'm bet you'll find Filipino native foods tasting. (But here in Phil. we do not fall forward dead face in it. Sorry. Only the joke!) Oh! Know! The <u>best</u> graduation gift I can receive is your to arrival in Davao. Though I know the impossible, I will say as we say here in Phil. that: Ang sarap pag ito ay totoo! (The better if it becomes true).

Now I must ask the priets' question w/c he ask me. Do you own your own house as well as your own car—i.e. have a house key and car key of your own? A Camaro or Firebird type car? The priets was worry coz your letter was too high level thinking, he said, coz he thinks then you are a philisoper in your letters (five) to me. He never cares you are not Roman catholic but he must know we love the other one & you don't say it in a letter. Only about the photoes & not good enough. Priets think Deep Mind is rage of devils but I told him your heartbroken life of love so he can understand you fight the devils hustle against you. Buttock & pointy part of heart, he was laughed. So I shouted down him in the church and cried and said I will take off my skirt and dash the street shouting Buttock and Pointy Part Father Narciso Laughed and Grabbed. So he got a long face and said Okay he approve if your letter next time say the Love of Me and have the money for plane journey ($1,000) back to Phil. if I am not made the happy wife of yours. So please, my darling! Do the right thing!

I enclose herewith one more picture me in the shower place of my sister house by my niece. I had borrow the negligee from my sister's drawer. So is secret but I got to give her (niece) P100 she will be quiet about you & me to her.

I wait your letter and the plans. I have no passport yet I think I can acquire that if we can come to agreement.

Always yours,

Luz

PS $1000 in <u>REGISTER</u> letter Please!

*

Gus's Hotel

East 12th and Ironbridge

Cleveland, Ohio, U.S.A.

 Sept. 1, 1991

Dearest Luz,

Sweetest Luz! Did I never say that I Love You? May I
fry in Hell for such an omission! What held my tongue
(my pen!) in the matter was my fear that you were just
toying with my imagination. But the negligee photo says
it all in more than simple words. I can see your nipples
underneath! I can see your nipples underneath! But I'm
afraid the pubic triangle—dare I bring such a thing up in
the presence of a virgin lady?—is obscured by a fold in the
fabric which, doubling or perhaps even trebling the thick-
ness, renders that sector of the print less than specific.
But I quibble. Your nipples would appear to be nearly the
bronze in hue of certain Roman coins minted ca. AD 81-
96 under Tribonerius Sextus. No books on numismatics
mention the comeliness of these specie of the time, but a
two asses (sing. as: a Roman bronze coin) denomination
coin I saw in the Colonial Arcade Coin Shop window last

year left me shivering, shaking all over. Deep Mind will be able to locate you now—though that will not be necessary. Read on!

But first, a few comments about my present circumstances for the priest's (watch your spelling, dear) information. At this time I have no house and must stay at Gus's Hotel in downtown Cleveland, but that will change when I am able to return to work full-time again. (My own home that I once shared with my Mother burned down years ago when it was hit by a falling satellite that had developed an insane passion for a Porn Queen who had been starring in Deep Mind at a period of deep loneliness for me. I don't smoke anymore, either.) And at this time I have no car and am wholly dependent on the Cleveland RTA (Rapid Transit Authority) for transportation, which is fine except for the danger of transvestites moving from the front of the bus to the back of the bus too many times without ever getting up during a single downtown loop trip, men dressed as women and upsetting the delicate balance of bipolars and resulting in a net hemorrhage loss of Universal Energy (entropy). You can tell they are men because they are so happy being women and smoothing down their whisker stubble in their compact mirrors. My driver's license was revoked the week after I raised the dead of America (July 4, 1976) when I was involved in a traffic accident at an intersection with cars operated by Gen. Francisco Franco and Pope Pius XII who were not injured at all but pointed accusing middle fingers at me for months afterward in Deep Mind Torture. So lately I have been looking at a used two-seater Textron E-Z-Go converted golf cart for sale by the owner. It is powered by six 12-volt automobile batteries and according to the owner can reach speeds of up to 14 mph and cover 36 miles between recharges. There is ample room in the back on the golf bag rack for 4 good-size bags of groceries and heavy duty straps to keep them from spilling out on the shoulder of the road (always a potential nightmare). The owner also said the same laws that govern Amish horse-and-buggies also govern golf carts on public thorough-fares. That is, you must have tail lights and not just reflectors here in Ohio. It is my hope someday to live out in the country and own one. Or am I just a wild dreamer?

No! I am Not! This week I purchased one round-trip ticket from the United States to Davao City, the Philippines, and back and one one-way ticket from Davao City to here for you, and I will arrive to gather you up on Oct. 28—after observing your graduation festivities, of course. I had been waiting for a formal invitation and finally got it in your last letter. I am enclosing a counter check for $200 for you to buy yourself a graduation gift and any early wedding preparations that may crop up. I had to put up my Ohio Teachers' Retirement Fund money for the plane ticket and Rudy at Liberty Bell Loans was not happy about it (he's ignorant) but he let me redeem my Mother's ring too. So everything is all set. I will await detailed instructions from you as to how and when we shall meet at the airport as I am not sure I will be able to recognize you fully clothed (Ha ha! Just a joke, like _you_ say). Just give me the word in your next letter. I await with baited breath.

Seriously, I Cannot But Love You. It has been so long for me to feel like this. Soon.

My Undying Love,
Harold

*

Office of Librarian
Southeastern Mindanao Teachers College
Davao City, Philippines
Oct. 28, 1991

Dear Harold Nitcombe Ill,

Hello! First of all, let me extend you my personal greetings. Formost let me tell you that I'm the sister of Luz who is writing you this letter and perhaps you'll be surprised why I'm writing you for the first time. Luz sometimes she talks astonishedly about you to me but I did not know if you gave a marriage promise of yourself to her.

But I will tell you just recently we had a family reunion (except our father missing) but unfortunately without our family knowledge Luz had eloped with her boyfriend whom we did not know any personal information of that man. Until this time we do not know any immediate information of her where abouts in this point of time except he manage the club where Luz was worked pt time at nights after quit SEMTCO (Southeastern Mindanao Teachers College) because of the low grades.

As you know a Filipino family had the culture of close family ties relationship unlike of the western culture. That's why, we are very concerned of her—we even helped and support each other but the problem is, she (Luz) is not helping herself very well, although she is very good sister. This event had made us worried. We found out that she is not serious & not helping herself in terms of employment especially now Philippines is in Economic recession.

My other sister was on the profession of teaching job & had strong effort helping her for education and employ-ment. But to her effort, she was in dismay because Luz is no longer available. As you know, Harold Ill, employment here in the Philippines is so very scarce. Philippine Economy has dropped & in crisis due to the effect of fear of kudeta & Political unstability. That's why, this year millions of employees both private and government will be laid off as one of the government measures to survive, sacraficing millions of employees will be jobless anytime soon. And I will tell you, I might be also affected fearing what shall I do? Probably I will decide to volunteer myself to work the domestic servant job in Hong Kong and the Singapore islands. But that is danger to my Virtue if I bend over wash a floor the Chinese wife is not at the home the husband try catch me en culo. We must hope for the best & also expect the worst.

Back to Luz, we think the man she had eloped with was a married man, that created a big problem to us. We know now why she did that because for sure she knows very much that the man she eloped with has no good standing or not credible to us because in the first place he is married & we dislike it very much and it is a crime to Philippine laws. We believe Luz has no plan to see us, because she knows that what she did was an embarrassing one & she's ashame to us that she could not face in person.

We belong to a Conservative family & we believe in Morality that we do not want our good reputation to be tainted with such kind of bad image. I'm sorry if I'm telling you this but I want to tell you about the things that had happened. If you have any question, please do not hesitate ask me.

I am writing to you so that you will not be wasting your time writing to her. To tell you frankly, we were not really pleased of what Luz was doing. I seems to think that she has no plan of doing good for her future, especially that she has a son in her pervious marriage. She married at the age of 17 & separated at the age of 20. The son is cute and raise by our mother in Bitauen province village.

Now I am writing also the condolences letter to other Luz penfriends because they are to be waiting the response of her to them but won't get them. There is nine (plus you) viz Mr. S. Bennekemper (Missouri, USA) Mr. L Skaarsgard (Stockholm, Swed.) Sgt. A Curtis (APO Japan) Mr E. Poe (Baltimore, USA) Dr. H. Herrero (Panama) Prof. A Piedersdorfer (Munchen, Germ.) Mr. Z. Obemeata (Lagos City, Nigeria) Mr. Lee (Seoul, S. Korea) etc

Harold Ill, that's all for now, but if you liked to make friend with me—exchanging idea, opinions, anything—I will appreciate it. I can write to you once in a while & could furnish you any information or development about Luz. I think, you really cared for her.

Little information about myself—I'm friendly typed,

educated, possessive a sense of humor, & easy to make laugh with & broad minded too, & with good manner and NO HANG UPS on that regard. And before I lest forget – an one man woman. TRUTH!

May God bless you,

Friendly yours,

Vera Lloren

PS May I ask you some question? Who shop your grocery for you and who do your laundry and ironing? Do you cook yourself? Or do you have a maid for these? Sorry to be nosey.

PSS "The essence of genious is <u>know</u> <u>what</u> <u>to</u> <u>overlook</u>" by William James. Vera

THE ONE TRACT MIND STORY
GIVE PISS A CHANCE

I *didn't hear the water running. You didn't wash your hands.*
Not that again.

Well you never learn.

Urine is sterile. I told you that.

Urine?

Piss, then.

Urine is such an ugly word. Piss is better. Pee is even better than that.

I agree. Did you know the Romans brushed their teeth with the stuff? To whiten them. It's in Catullus.

I know. Ammonia. Like bleach.

Right. They especially prized Spanish piss. It got even stronger on the long journey to Rome.

Tell me something.

What's that?

Well, did you ever taste the stuff? I mean do as the Romans did?

Nope. Never even tempted.

Okay.

Okay what?

Can I ask you a personal question?

That one was personal enough. But go ahead.

It's a little—I don't know—

Try me.

Well, did you ever pee in a woman's mouth?

What a question!

Well?

Sure. Once.

Really? You really did?

Once. Like I said.

Did you pay her or something?

She came into the bathroom. Knelt down beside me while I was about to take a wizz.

How did you know what she wanted?

She just sort of sat there on her knees.

Looking up into your eyes like a puppy? Or staring at your dick?

I don't remember. It was a long time ago.

But you knew what she wanted.

It was strange. She didn't say anything. I didn't either.

But you knew what she wanted? Like telepathy?

I did.

And?

It was the closest I've ever felt to being back inside the womb.

More like peeing in a swimming pool, I'd say. Like a kid.

It was a kind of quiet ecstasy. Just an easy release. A sort of blissful helplessness. I could have been asleep.

What was her name?

I don't remember now.

But you remember pissing in her mouth. You remember that.

It's the one thing about her I never forgot.

You said it's sterile. Urine's really sterile?

That's what the books say.

And she swallowed it—all of it?

She emptied me.

But you don't remember her name?

I don't.

That's disgusting. That's the part that's so disgusting.

I'm sorry.

That's okay. I just hate it when men don't remember what we do for them.

*

I'm sorry but I have to ask you something.

What's that?

That woman you told me—

Oh brother.

I'm sorry. I can't get her out of my head.

Just forget about it. It's not imp—

What—was she a stripper or something—or a hooker.

No. And I told you I didn't pay her.

Well what then? That's all I want—

I said forget about it. I never should—

I just want to know. I mean was she a little mentally off? I know some guys like—

She was a teacher.

A teacher! My God!

Third grade. And remarkably sane as far as I could tell.

She taught children!

Still does probably.

What could possibly possess her—to drink urine?

Urine?

Piss. Pee. It's all the same.

That's not what you said yesterday.

Yesterday I thought maybe you were pulling my leg. Like you always like to do. I was just playing along. Now I've had time to think about it.

Oh?

I mean why. What's the thrill?

Thrill? Who said anything about a thrill? I didn't—

You said you really enjoyed it. Got off on it. Back in the womb and all that shit.

Maybe I did. But I didn't say anything about how *she* felt about it. Thrill, no I don't think so.

She must have said something. *You don't do something like that and not—say anything. I can't believe that.*

Well . .

She did say something! I knew it!

Darling . .

What did she say. Tell me.

She said I reminded her of her father.

What!

She said I reminded her of her father. Something about my eyes.

Your eyes? What in the hell does that mean?

She told me when she was younger. In high school. Her father was dying of cancer. At home. In their house. Her mother wouldn't touch the old man. Hated him, or some such shit.

Go on.

And on top of all that, he had a stroke. Couldn't—you know—take care of himself. Became, what's the word— incontinent.

I don't think I want to hear this.

And her mother wouldn't do anything for him. So *she* had to.

This isn't funny. Yesterday you were funny. But this isn't funny.

So she had to clean up after him. Get him to the bathroom if she could. Sometimes she couldn't. His bowel movements were no problem—came out in hard little chunks.

She told you about this?

Hard little chunks. But his urine—

Stop right now. Stop right now. I don't believe a word of this. I don't want to listen to this. You're making this all up. To get back at me for something.

So she started drinking it. Don't ask me why. Saved—I don't know—time. I found it unbelievable too.

Saved time? You're insane. You're the one who's insane.

She said it brought her closer to him after a while. It's complicated. I know. She said there had always been a distance between them. And she had always wanted to close it. And this—

This is a joke, isn't it? There's a punchline coming. I know it.

Nope.

Tell me there's a punchline coming. This is all bullshit. This is just one of your sicko standup routines you're trying out on me, isn't it.

You wanted to know. You're the one who wanted to know.

She said you reminded her of her father. That's the punchline, isn't it. What a sick joke. What a sick punchline.

Okay. It's a joke. A sick joke. Whatever. Sorry.

Tell me it's all a joke. Yesterday and today. Tell me.

I just did.

Okay. Now listen. If she told you all this you must remember her name. I can't believe you don't remember that.

Of course I remember.

What is it then? What is it?

Can't you just give it a break. Maybe a guy shouldn't piss and tell, you know. That's all.

Oh brother. Oh brother. Don't try and joke yourself out of this one. Don't you dare!

Darling . .

What is it? Tell me what it is. Then maybe I'll believe you. And don't make up something stupid like Miss Saffron Pease.

You know who she is. You went to high school with her.

High school? I did? Who— Her father die— High school— Cance— Stro— Yes— HER? That stuck up bitch! HER! That insufferable snob! HER! How we hated that arrogant— Looking down on all of us all the time. That's hilarious! Disgusting! I can't believe it! That's rich.

That's just so rich! I love it! Tell me it's not true! It can't be— My God, darling. Oh I so hope it's true!

Well, it's true enough.

And you liked it!

I guess I can live without it.

It was just a one time thing, right? I mean—

Just a one time thing, yes.

Before we—

Before we started seeing each other. Yes.

That arrogant slut! That whore! She always . .

Always what?

Your eyes. She looked up into your eyes. Not at your dick. She looked up into your eyes.

I don't remember. Like I said. It was a long time ago.

I can't— I can't look into your eyes—without—

Without—what?

Without—

Without—what a funny word.

Without thinking!

Without thinking what, darling?

That she loved it too.

THE MAGICAL REALISM STORY
MAI KEE

They gathered in the hour before noon every day on the scuffed sofas and worn leatherette armchairs in the lobby of the hotel and waited for the tour director to show up and go over the day's schedule. Every one of them had a tale to tell of the night before and a bar to recommend. "At Pussy Galore, Steve. There's this girl who inserts darts into her—" "Can uncap a bottle of Coke with one quick pelvic thr—" "—with this fucking eel, Al, I couldn't believe—" There were, by my count, a dozen of them: a blond and ruddy hail-fellow-well-met type who looked like he coached girls' softball back in the States; an ex-hippie of indeterminate years with an enviable mane of ashy blond hair and a doughy, seamed face, like gently folded batter; the dapper Southerner called "Doc" who made no secret of the pills he washed down with quick slugs of Pepsi; a Viet Nam vet who wore a light-weight hiker's vest everywhere he went and claimed a special bond with Southeast Asia that no one else could possibly fathom; the designated asshole of the group, a redhead of about thirty with the meticulously trimmed beard of a junior naval officer who incessantly intruded into conversations with puerile allusions to the size of his cock, "Mr.

Moby Dick"; a semi-retired bailbondsman whose advice to his tour mates on all matters pecuniary was an emphatic and succinct "Buy Debt! There'll be a check in your mailbox every month!"; an octogenarian former professor of rocketry of Teutonic stock who, to my knowledge, never once uttered a word to anyone except Hummel, the tour director, and then only in hushed, brief asides; and maybe a half dozen others, all fiftyish and paunchy as yours truly, and to each and every man jack of them his own peculiar kink: trout flies, Tonka trucks, tutus.

I sat across the lobby from them on these late mornings, inconspicuous in my tropical khakis, feigning absorption in the splashy brochures available on the tourism counter, listening, daring to jot down a phrase or two of conversation when a word or image struck a note. The drawn, weathered Thai woman with the dime-size chocolate mole on her forehead behind the reception desk attended dutifully to a clipboard and issued perfunctory instructions to the chambermaids as they trundled up to the desk to collect the room keys of the late risers. It was all business to her and her drudges. She batted not an eyelash whenever one of the group erupted with an observation on the previous night's forays into the fleshpots of Patpong or Soi Cowboy or Nana's Plaza.

"I tell you she had one," insisted the ruddy girls' softball coach.

"And I'm telling you you're nuts, Jack," the one called Doc countered with peppy finality, swigging on his Pepsi. "There's no such thing as—"

"If she did," Designated Asshole interjected, "you'd've been a fool to let her slip away like that. If you were a man you'd still be upstairs right now in your room with your wick in—"

"I think she had to go to the dentist this morning," Jack defended himself. "She's very quiet. Never says a word. A toothache or someth—"

At this the entire group burst into a shower of derisive guffaws.

"The dentist!"

"A toothache!"

"Buddy, if she's got teeth inside there you're lucky you're not in surgery right—"

"You sure your last name's not Bobbit!"

"Ha! Fucking is probably just her way of flossing!"

"Jack, I'll tell you what," offered the rotund bailbondsman with the trout-fly-nipple fetish. "Ask her out to lunch and if she starts shoveling food under her skirt—"

"Well," snapped Jack, his ruddy moon-face flushing deeply. "I know what I *know*."

"It's possible, you know," the ex-hippie declared,

searching the eyes of the others with an anxious New Age proselytizing zeal. "I met a guy who sighted a Vu Quang ox in Cambodia last year. He was as close to it as I am to that guy over there." He pointed at me and I casually retracted the tip of my ballpoint pen with a discrete pump of my thumb.

"Shit," sniffed the Viet Nam vet in the hiker's vest. "Anything's possible in this part of the world. In Nam some of the whores put razor blades up their pussies. They were working for Charlie. A guy would take her up to her room and jump her bones and *zip!* the head of his dick would come out looking like a bloody radish rosette."

The Viet Nam vet and the ex-hippie locked glances, unlikely allies in Jack's defense. Only the morning before I'd listened to their brief, heated exchange about Nixon's invasion of Cambodia and the torching of the ROTC building at Kent State. Today they were delivered from the awkwardness of sharing sides by the arrival of the tour director, a lanky man assembled utterly in contrasting shades of gray—slacks, shirt, socks, watchband, hair, eyes, down to the twin sheaves of quills bristling out of his nostrils—like camouflage for a descent into an ashheap. He had very bad teeth—gray, naturally—and long, nervous fingers and a striking Thai woman with liquid, molten eyes in tow. She was darker even than the rural village girls who flooded down from the impoverished northern provinces to work in bars called Pussy Alive and Baby A-Go-Go and Bunny House. The tour director introduced the woman as Poom and let the group know she'd be guiding those who wanted to take in an afternoon of *muay thai*. Blank stares hung in the air all around until Hummel explained, "Kick-boxing. It's the national sport here. Like baseball back home." At which point the group swung its collective head in the direction of Poom. But Designated Asshole had already taken her aside and was looking down on her meaningfully, once or twice giving her elbow a pat with the cupped palm of his hand.

*

Jack, it appeared, was my man. Of course it was more than possible that what he took to be a *mai kee*—certainly he had never heard the term before—was just a love muscle, the overdeveloped *constrictor vaginae* you can find represented in almost any human female population from Burton's Abyssinia to Malnikoff's Aleutians if you look hard enough. There was no reason to assume he had any expertise. Men are astonished all the time by what a woman can learn to do with the right regimen of contraction exercises or the proper spring-loaded device ordered by catalog from the Euphoria Collection or Vibrator XXX-press. Ask Dr. Ruth.

And there have been hoaxes. The "Snapping Pussies of Lamu'u-nika" scandal in the late 1930's was a case in point—with its outrageous rumors of voracious *vaginae dentatae* devouring whole native villages grass huts and all just as the globe was about to be sucked into the maelstrom of another world war—and suggests that in times of social and political upheaval the human psyche is quite capable of projecting its deepest fears on the nightmarish screen of tabloid headlines. One did not, at the risk of one's own sanity and safety and reputation, go traipsing across the globe in search of the merely sensational. Poor, hapless Federsen and Wohl, trapped in the crocodile-infested lowlands of Lamu'u-nika just as the Japanese Imperial Army "liberated" the island's capital from its colonial overlords.

Yes, there have been hoaxes. Occasions for knowing titters and sly winks, in retrospect: the "Snapping Pussies of Lamu'u-nika" sham with its subtle overtones of castration anxiety was the Piltdown Man and Cardiff Giant of the Freudian Era rolled into one. But Jack knew what he knew, as he said. And it would have been folly for me to take him *cum grano salis* after so many mornings and afternoons of sitting around lobbies of two-star hotels listening to realtors from Spokane and purchasing agents from Albany compare prices and performances and tits and muffs. That the others in his group considered him a bit off his ruddy, moon-faced head was fortuitous. Frankly, I wanted him shimmed away from the pack just a tad, if possible. The more likely he would gravitate toward "his" girl. And the sooner. And I on his heels. Human psychology is funny. These male tour groups were spontaneous, makeshift societies in miniature. Members forged tribal bonds the first couple of days of knocking around Bangkok together, wisecracking and sharing confidences and exploits, masking their fundamental unworldliness with a shared good-old-homeboy skepticism: "I'm telling you, Jack, such women don't . ."

Jack joined the *muay thai* contingent as it followed Poom single file out the hotel doors. Coal Black, I thought, and Her Seven Moral Dwarves: Horny, Lusty, Randy, Rutty, Humpy, Rammy and Doc, who had switched his wash from Pepsi to Singha beer with suave prestidigitation. Two others followed a street kid who claimed he knew the best place in Bangkok to buy bespoke silk shirts. "No reep-off, meester. You come tailor today," the kid lied. "Ready tomorrow." The trout-fly-nipple fetish bailbondsman and the Viet Nam vet discovered they had something in common—they liked selecting girls from a gallery of choices—and set off for a massage parlor whose glossy fliers promised miniskirted masseuses seated on tiers and foam lavings on air-mattresses. Designated Asshole alone remained seated in the empty lobby.

"You're not interested in *muay thai*?" I ventured from across the lobby, folding my brochure in my lap.

"Seen it. Last time I was here."

"You've been to Bangkok before?"

"Third time."

"I take it you like it here."

"The girls are too small. That's my problem," he complained and shot me a look of imperial condescension. "Even the ones who have had a kid."

"My."

Designated Asshole stroked his red beard. He had fine blue eyes with tiny pupils and a narrow, unimpressive chest. It was difficult not to glance down at his crotch seam to surmise if everything there were as grandly appointed as he would have others believe.

"You fellows were pretty hard on your buddy this morning."

"There's one like him every year on these tours. Some guy thinks he's discovered the most unique bit of gash on the planet. Then two days later he's waltzing in the hotel with a new girl. Then *she's* the most unique bit of gash on the planet . ."

"Well, what was so unique about this one, if I may ask?"

"Hah! Listen to this. He claims the girl has a *tongue* inside her cunt. So it's like getting laid and a blow job all in one."

"A tongue," I said.

"Can you believe that? Of course," he pulled up a bit, raising his eyebrows and shrugging, "maybe she had some special action down there. But a tongue! The poor guy probably just hasn't been laid right and proper in a while."

"A tongue," I repeated. "A *mai kee*?"

"Pardon?"

"Nothing. Just rambling."

"You don't believe—"

"Of course not. Poor guy, like you say."

Designated Asshole was still staring at me through the filmy glass doors of the Hotel Sukhumvit as I hopped a tuk-tuk—that onomatopoeic and ubiquitous motorized three-wheeled contrivance with maniacally suicidal U-turn impulses and murderous fumes—and directed the driver to take me to Banglamphu. Waiting around the hotel lobby had given me an appetite, but my finances forbade me little more than a bowl of Banglamphu street stall noodles for lunch these days. Fieldwork, after all, can be expensive, especially for an independent. But Bangkok can be a magical city, whatever kind of budget you're stuck with. One morning you are fishing a snake out of your toilet and the next week you are wolfing down chicken and rice at the wedding of an Israeli backpacker named Schlomo and a Thai Muslim bar girl named Sumalee. There are some four hundred Buddhist temples in Bangkok—featuring the fifty-yard-long Reclining Buddha, the mysterious and untouchable Emerald Buddha, and the five-and-a-half-ton Solid Gold Buddha—and many times that many prostitutes in the bars of Patpong and Soi Cowboy and Nana's Plaza ministering to pilgrims whose reverence leans more toward the enchantments of the flesh than the incantations of the spirit. Indeed, there's something for everyone. Pirates from the South China Sea and dentists from Waukegan will find themselves warmly received at a Patpong hole-in-the-wall bar called Pussy Jolly Roger, where the girls dance naked with miniature Captain Hook hats on their heads and white plastic molars glued to their nipples. Their "tooth pasties."

*

The only documented *mai kee* on record is a woman from the town of That Phanom in the northeastern Thai province of Isan. And scanty documentation that was: a letter dated some thirty years ago from Michael Fishbourne to one of his graduate students back home in the States. In it he mentions almost in passing that a 37-year-old woman referred to only as Noi was capable of extraordinary feats of dexterity involving her "nether region." These included the production of sounds that were "most human-like." The expulsion of air from the vagina is, of course, hardly a rare thing and seldom silent, as impassioned lovers know only too well, and serious scholars dismissed his claim as simply a trick and a delusion. He had, after all, he later admitted, *paid* the woman for a private demonstration.

And Fishbourne was grieving, in those days, the death of a beloved wife. One of his colleagues pointed out that when her cancer was in its final, virtually untreatable stage, Fishbourne had carted her off to a psychic surgeon in the Philippines and believed that the relatively comfortable last six months of her life were directly attributable to the mass of liverish material the "surgeon" had removed from her abdomen. Poor Fishbourne, people said. He had always been such a rigorous man. And now pursuing phantoms in the backwaters of Southeast

Asia. Nevertheless, Fishbourne claimed he had examined the Isan woman after her performance and used the word "glossa" to describe an unusual structure he was certain was involved in the enunciation of the most distinctive of the sounds: *mai kee.* Forty years passed since that letter was posted and no one gave it another thought, save for the occasional cocktail party joke (one party—there was pot on hand—finally broke up into uncontrollable giggles when everyone realized they could not begin a sentence with anything other than the word *Mikey*) at the long-dead professor's expense, until Political Correctness and Sexual Harassment Codes put an end to even that last little shred of immortality.

And then two years ago I arrived in Bangkok on a wholly other mission. The UN wanted expert "classifiers" to decide which of the refugees streaming across the Thai-Cambodian-Laotian borders were true political refugees and which ones were just looking for a free lunch. The job was a cinch. Everybody was hungry. Ergo they were all refugees. From hunger, anyway. The UN didn't see it that way. I was dismissed. My university department head wrote me a curt letter letting me know my "unprofessionalism" had jeopardized its standing with some important international programs and that I needn't hurry back. They even dredged up the old Fishbourne business.

As a lark, weary of the bad food and beetles and tedious humdrum of life along the Laotian border, I published a brief article in an obscure magazine back in the States titled "The Talking Pussy of That Phanom." I had not expected anybody back at Harvard would see it. But people are quite cutthroat in their vigilance around universities these days and they keep their eyes peeled. It was a joke, really, the article. Though you do hear things upcountry, talk. Thai rurals are an outgoing folk, especially when they get hopped up on the local hooch. And, truth to tell, back in the day, I was that grad student. I had liked old Fishbourne, cranky and supercilious as he could sometimes be. It hurt me that my mentor's name had become synonymous with "delusion" and "gullibility." "Keep your head about you," people dehorted jocularly at the airport as they shook hands and bade farewell to colleagues embarking on journeys that would take them deep into Stone Age turf. "Don't let those Ifugao *fishbourne* you."

*

From the bar of the Sukhumvit I could see directly into the lobby where the group would be gathering to launch their evening sorties on the bars of Patpong. I regretted having spoken to Designated Asshole. It had been inexcusable and unnecessary. I hadn't needed any confirmation of what Jack claimed he "knew." That was my job to verify it. And I didn't want anyone to get wind of what I was up to. I had let one—my one and only—slip through my fingers six months before by loosening my lips too readily to a Delhi arms merchant at the bar of Pussy See Pussy Do. It had never crossed my mind that the guy might take me seriously, so much bemused condescension had I endured at the hands of *farangs* I'd bellied up to the bar with over the past year and a half. Or that he might want sweet little Pong for himself. And have the bucks to spirit her out of the country overnight right under my nose. What a fool I'd been! He had even told me he was a Collector of Oddities. A goat with three eyes. A shell-less tortoise. Conspiratorially he intimated he had a line on a Vu Quang ox calf. Only three ever captured, and two of them died within months. A sort of Southeast Asian unicorn. Poor Pong.

And for a while there I was beginning to get a reputation. "See that Yank over there. That's the guy who's looking for a girl with a tongue in her pussy." "Hey, Mr. Harry. You see that girl dancing in red bikini? Tag say Number 46. She got a tongue in she's pussy. She my friend. You pay she bar fine. 600 *baht*. Take me too. 600 another *baht*."

"Hey, Sir Grandfather Big Nose. You want girl got tongue in she's pussy? You put you's in mine! Ha ha ha!"

So I had to lay low from ridicule for a while, if only for the sake of my dignity. And take stock of my finances. The fact is that if you want to get inside a Thai whore's quim and loll your finger or tongue or pecker around it's going to cost you on average 2000 *baht* a pop. That's real money at today's exchange rate. And then you figure at best, at the very best, maybe one in five hundred might be a *mai kee.* Say fifty bucks times five hundred girls is better than twenty-five grand. Of course you could get lucky and find one your first month or your first week or even your first day. But that's the stuff of fiction and lottery dreams. And I suspect the ratio is closer to one in two thousand. (Don't even reach for your calculator here—you haven't got that much in the bank.) One in two thousand is a guess, naturally. There's no way to tell. I made an appointment one afternoon with a gynecologist at one of the V.D. clinics on Patpong. I figured if anyone had come into contact with that many vaginas it would have to be a Patpong woman's doctor. But this woman's doctor turned out to be a woman doctor decidedly unsympathetic to abstruser avenues of inquiry. "Crazy *farang*!" "Crazy foreigner!" Let's just be generous and say that that branch of medical science is still in its infancy over here.

And then, during this respite, I came up with the grand scheme. Beautiful. Right out of thin air. These budget sex tour groups. Twelve, fifteen, sometimes twenty men (and curiously, now and again, the odd wife). Say fifteen guys times ten days at one girl a day comes out to, what, one hundred and fifty girls. Nearly half a year's research for one working alone on limited funds. All I had to do was hang out in the hotel lobbies and do a little harmless eavesdropping. Gents who back in Indianapolis would never own up to ever even having chatted with a hooker would carry on with expansive good cheer about the Patpong whore they had bedded the night before. And, as often as not, in lurid, polychrome detail. Of course, as I say, there was no way of knowing if Jack could tell the difference between a genuine *mai kee* and simply a gifted, well-trained pubococcygeal. Not many men can, I suppose. That, in the end, was my job.

The tour director arrived without Poom this evening and took a quick head count. All born this side of the Great War were present or accounted for: Doc and his white pills and Singha wash, apparently, would not be bound by clock time and had already hit the streets of Patpong. One chair sat ominously empty of its usual occupant. But only now did this absence intrude on the jovial anticipation of the punters. In the stillness that spread out from the lobby even unto my stool in the bar could be heard the soft rapping of the black velvet knuckles of the actuarial glove. Buy Debt of the trout-fly-nipple fetish and a slack-jawed office manager from Baltimore leaned toward each other and conferred in whispers. Designated Asshole examined his fingernails and checked his watch. The rest stared at Hummel or into their laps.

"Has anyone seen Professor Wunderlich?"

Nobody had.

Then the Nam vet and the ex-hippie spoke up simultaneously. They had the rooms on either side of the octogenarian's on the third floor and had helped the old man fit his key into his lock when he came back tipsy the previous night with a sixteen-year-old bar-fined out of Pussy Delight on one arm and a sullen Lao missing an earlobe on the other. He hadn't come down for the noon meeting, but that wasn't unusual. And if anyone had the right to sleep in, it was the professor.

"I'll just give his room a ring," announced the tour director in a sort of public whisper, and walked over to the house phone on the reception desk. The poor guy. A corpse, of course, is a tour director's worst nightmare. There would be the embassy to notify. And the police. And what passed in the tropical Third World for a coroner and morgue. The outlay for a casket and the shipment Stateside. Thirty years ago when they shipped Fish-bourne home, with no next of kin, I volunteered to drive out to the airport and claim the remains. They asked me to identify him right there at Customs. Handed me a sur-gical mask and ushered me into a small room and popped open the sealed coffin with a vacuum *whoosh*. His face was puffed and purple, as if his head were in the process of metamorphosing into a huge plum. His dentures were gone. Probably melted down, I realize now, and cast into a souvenir gold ring for a GI on R and R from a war just a mortar heave away in the rice paddies of the Mekong Delta.

With the receiver tucked between his shoulder and ear, Hummel stared dismally for some minutes at the clasp of his gray watchband. He set the phone back in its cradle and, as if he had locked in place a new fuse and completed a magic circuit, the doors of the lobby elevator cranked open and out ambulated the professor with the bar-fine from Pussy Delight at his side. Hummel grinned in almost cosmic relief and steepled his hands together and nodded in a mock-Thai bow. The Lao—she indeed was missing an earlobe—floated down the stairway moments later. Many of the new arrivals, particularly the hill girls, feared and distrusted elevators. Escalators too, I'd learned the hard way, having spent a good quarter of an hour in a department store one afternoon urging an upcountry Isan girl (she hailed from a village near That Phanom and I had hoped she might know a bit of *mai kee* lore) to "just step forward and grab the handrail" while the pretty young clerks in their spotless uniform dresses at the perfume counter sniggled uncontrollably behind cupped palms. And finally, when Nok got the hang of it, I had to drag her out of the store bodily, so fascinated had she become with riding the "walky ladder."

With the professor of rocketry now a securely identified blip on the tour director's screen—often at these meetings I observed his head swing around evenly in the manner of a radar scanner to keep track of his "boys"—Hummel instructed the group to rendezvous on Patpong at the flashy, neon-decked Pussy Royale. He would send them off two by two in tuk-tuks from the streetcorner outside the Sukhumvit. From the Pussy Royale he was to lead them to the night's special destination, Carabao House, a cozy upstairs nook specializing in oral delights. He had struck a deal with the mama-san and they would have the place all to themselves for two hours. "All girls in the buff and no tipping expected." A paragraph in his brochure I had found stuffed behind a cushion of a lobby sofa promised an "orgy of tongues, tit, and twat" and apparently this was the golden night. But Hummel was a careful man, too. Although Patpong would be teeming with thousands of pleasure-seekers, he knew better than to arrive there in the mini-bus in which he ferried his charges to the alligator farm or their afternoon of *muay thai*. Mini-buses meant tours and a stop at Patpong meant "sex tour" and it was no secret the local police chief would want his palm greased to overlook so brazen a flaunting of the country's laws. Sex tours are illegal in Thailand the way drug rings are illegal in the States—"Like, yeh, right, man." One group I'd followed two months before ignored this nicety of the judiciously placed bribe and the tour director found himself being interviewed on CNN—from a jail cell. So off the group went two by two in their tuk-tuks.

I hopped in a tuk-tuk at a stand across the street and instructed the driver *Ka-roo-na nam phom pai yang Pat-pong*. I paid up front and tossed in an extra ten baht. *Reh-o*, I urged. "Quickly. Short cut." The Carabao House arrangement was an unanticipated snag. My hope was for Jack to make a bee-line from the Pussy Royale to the bar where "his girl" worked. It was possible there would be as many as thirty or forty girls dancing there and I wanted him to lead me right to her. I didn't want to spend a couple hours outside Carabao House while Hummel's crew sat around with their pants down to their ankles and got their collective wad siphoned off. Worse, once fellated my man might decide he had had his share of libidinous play for the evening and spend the rest of the night tooling up and down the strip bouncing bottles of Singha off his lips.

*

Pussy Royale was a newly-remodeled showcase with a huge rectangular bar that took up nearly all its interior space save for the barstools and the row of snuggle couches along each wall where, for the price of a "lady's drink," you could tweak a waitress's bare boobs and trade such vital information as your Christian name, your nationality—avoid anywhere that sounds even remotely "Arabic"—and whether you want head and she gives it—"smokes," in the local slang—or not. A dart show was in progress as I entered. A girl lay naked on her back on the raised dance floor inside the bar firing tiny pointed projectiles from her nether cleft at a cluster of colored balloons tied to a pole. Blow-gun style. Pop. She was accurate. Popopop. Western women especially tend to look down their noses at these kinds of displays. But it is the sort of pointless talent men of all cultures—raised to appreciate the absurd skills required to win foolhardy playground dares and daffy barroom wagers—find eminently admirable. We've been competitors since we were australopithecines, and we've never been able to shake it. And it's certainly more entertaining than watching some gladiatrix of an Olympic archer from South Korea with a high-tech bow that looks like a scaled down space shuttle console sling cupidinous bolts at a calibrated bull's eye. But it will be a long, long time before we see a trio of Patpong girls empedestalled on the stepped platform of an Olympic awards ceremony to accept the gold, silver and bronze in Pussy-Blow-Dart-Pop-Balloon as the Thai flag is unfurled overhead and the national anthem pipes through the stadium's speaker system. And this is unfair, as the world of sport's only real moral claim on our wallets and enthusiasms has always been the promise of equal opportunity to the disenfranchised and unempowered. Imagine, if you will, snapping open tomorrow's sports pages and coming across this:

P-B-D-P-B TAKES FIRST OLYMPIC STEP

Monaco (Reuters) — Pussy-Blow-Dart-Pop-Balloon took a first step toward eventual inclusion in the Olympic Games when it was granted provisional recognition by the International Olympic Committee (IOC) Monday.

But hopeful P-B-D-P-B sharpshooters can expect no

smooth trajectory to the Summer Games, IOC Director General Septimus "Sept" Bladder warned.

The governing body of the newly recognized sport–the International Pussy-Blow-Dart-Pop-Balloon Association–will first have two years in which to convince IOC members of their claim to full recognition.

If successful, they would join 17 other non-Olympic sports waiting hopefully on the sidelines for the chance to ..

But forgive me: it is a curious habit of the expat mind at bar to editorialize to itself at length on matters of little consequence to the World-at-Large.

Members of the tour group trickled into Pussy Royale and gathered at a corner of the bar just as the dart show came to a close and a string of dancers mounted the stage in red or yellow or black bikini bottoms but no tops. The panties would stay on for a while–pinned to them were plastic tags with the girls' identification numbers–and come off as the girls neared the end of their half hour shift. With, of course, your stunning exception, the less they wore the more they looked alike. But I oversimplify. From eye-level at the bar two distinct types emerge. The girls with longer, prominent pubic bones, exposed, hard-nosed, defiant cunts promising a furiously demanding fuck that will end with one agonist's shoulders firmly pinned to the mat. (Not recommended, you understand, for the cardiacally impaired. Every year, according to the German Embassy, some dozen or so overweight male Kraut tourists pop a couple hundred milligrams of Viagra and blow out their tickers as bedsprings groan and then subside in baleful silence.) And their meeker counterparts, the smaller pubises that seem neatly tucked away, barely v-shaped at all, soft, puellesque, shyly hinting at a gentle, swaying lay that dissolves at climax into childlike giggles. There are sub-types too, naturally, and that occasional stunner that defies all classification. But one man's meat is another man's *poisson*, as the French say. If you ever want to hear two men disagree on the transcendent merits of what is right smack there in front of them, take them to Patpong.

The tour boys, jovial and backslapping now that they were out on the town again, attracted the attention of girls seeking a "lady's drink." Foreigners in playful high spirits can be generous. A "lady's drink," little more than a couple ounces of orange juice or cola in a tumbler of ice, runs about 150 to 200 *baht*—say five bucks—of which the girl is given a share. At closing time, or before she leaves with the customer who has "bar fined" her out for the night, she cashes in a handful of plastic chips—one for each drink she has hustled–that the bartender has doled out to her that evening. The girls, I knew, avoided the quiet loner, nursing a beer and sulking, his solitary thoughts focused on that whore he had once had long ago and now, through the warped prism of memory melded to imagination, has become the ideal against whom all the pretty tarts working the crowd and hustling drinks are measured and fall short, his dashed hopes breeding in him a stinginess that is but another face of despair. Such a loner they took me to be, I suppose, and in the twenty minutes I had been sitting at the bar across from the tour group boys, only one bothered to approach my barstool perch, and she backed away in stunned bafflement when I snapped at her, apropos of nothing at all, the last phrase I remembered studying in my copy of Cricket Knight's *Thai Spoken With a Smile: "Maeng-ka-phroon! Ra-wang!"* ("Jellyfish! Be careful!")

And then Jack made his move. He slid off his barstool, spoke into Hummel's ear under the disco music, and headed toward the exit. I tucked some bills into the tiny wooden barrel set in front of me that held my tab, and shimmied and wove my way through the yammering shoals of grinning, cajoling Brits and Aussies and Frogs and Krauts and Yanks and turbanned Sub-continent Ivy MBA's. Jack's chin sawed through the crowd with gritty determination. He had forsworn the Carabao House orgy and could only be headed for his *mai kee*. There is a thrill that all men know at least once in their lives–even the tender-footed urbanite who has never cradled a shotgun–when the certainty that his prey is about to reveal itself comes as a scent, almost an intuition, a sweet chill to the bone. So it was with me.

*

Pussy Hard Rock was an upstairs bar of the shabbier sort. Some twenty or twenty-five girls altogether, a third of them "dancing," each bending her knees in time to the music and, catching a customer's eye, lowering her pelvic cradle into a squat and producing a bump or two and a counter-clockwise circular rump grind. When you first enter one of these places, your mind takes a moment to adjust to the circumstances as your eyes sweep the room and your heart does a little jig to syncopate its beat to the rawness and rhythm of flesh and sound. Encoded in the hetero male brain is a triangle-shaped hole into which only a triangular peg will fit. The deltoid female pubic muff and the mound of soft adipose flesh on which it flourishes is that triangular peg. The ancient Greeks intuited this and squandered the intellectual capital of an entire civilization waxing poetic and mystical about triangles in weird paeans to a Realm of Forms. The Pythagorean Theorem has to be the wackiest statement of erotic longing of all time—save perhaps for the Willendorf Venus. Had these eminences taken their minds off of Platonic Love for a moment and balanced their isosceles on its point rather than allowing it to rest so dully and securely on its base, perhaps they would have seen this. And I won't even go into the matter of old Imhotep and his Pyramids. Suffice it to say that when our species shed the matted hair from its back and chest and limbs and stood up so nakedly and brazenly straight, the triangular muff remained, a signal detectable across distances, stripped down and sleeked up as we were for speed and agility and general mayhem on the broad African savannahs.

Jack sat on a barstool ensorcelled by a dancer with a thumbnail-sized bit of pubic hair that covered little more than her tiny crevasse. Barely five-foot, skin that achingly lovely bronze that pallid Westerners bake themselves for days on end under fitful suns to attain, she was an Alpha female in the best Southeast Asian sense of the term—not a cigarette burn or razor blade scar on her. She dipped into a squat and performed a couple of jocular, mock-seductive writhes for Jack. She had a wide smile and two rows of even, baby-like teeth almost identical in size. She pointed at her cheek and rolled her eyes, a reference, I took it, to her morning trip to the dentist.

As she rose up out of her squat and brought her knees together, her thighs touched, just barely, leaving a tiny open space at her divine fulcrum through which flitted a splash of unearthly white light. And then something happened. A strange and dark rage, like a fever unannounced by any other symptoms, flushed through me instantly, subsided, and left my limbs swamped and leaden. A film of condensed vapors like gelid sweat bathed the roots of my hair as the floor under me gave with the spongy elasticity of a trampoline. I staggered a few steps to my left and collapsed on one of the empty snuggle couches along the wall and gaped helplessly at Jack and then at his girl and then at Jack again. A plump waitress in bikini bottoms and a flimsy negligee jacket homed in on me and I managed to order a bottle of Singha, shooing her away with a feeble, breathless *Maeng-ka-phroon! Ra-wang!* when she returned with the beer and tried to hustle herself a 200 *baht* lady's drink. I put the bottle to my lips and as I tipped it up caught again a glance of that trigonal postage stamp of black fur and the light that danced just beneath it. The hot flash of fevered rage descended again and I closed my eyes in abject submission. Pools of iridescent blue dots and shimmering red dots swirled into each other and separated out again. The driving beat of "Gimme Shelter" pressed in on my diaphragm like a bunched fist and I sucked in gulps of the bar's machine-chilled air: *It's just a kiss away, it's just a kiss away.* The fear that I might possibly be truly physically sick hit and–to try to get a grip on a reality that seemed about to abandon me to a bottomless Void–I blindly ran through an inventory of afflictions tropical and otherwise that might strike so out of the blue: Malaria. Hepatitis. Typhus. Cholera. Coronary. Black Clap. Allergy. Acid flashback. Male menop—

"You okay, pal?"

I opened my eyes. Jack's blond moon-face swayed over me, searching and concerned, as if suspended on an invisible guy-wire.

"You don't look so good."

*

I stayed in bed three days straight, getting up only to use the toilet and boil myself bowls of bland white noodles. I sent my landlady's son to a Chinese herbalist with a request for something that would soothe "overwrought nerves" and he returned with an envelope filled with a grainy brown meal that was apparently some sort of "tea." I steeped this and drank it and did feel a little better. On the fourth day I rose and dressed and walked shakily downstairs to use the lobby phone of the lodging house. The desk clerk at the Sukhumvit–the parched woman with the dime-sized chocolate mole, I assumed–replied archly in high-pitched screechy tones that Mr. Hummel's group had left for Don Muang International Airport the previous morning. I had wanted to thank Jack for putting me in a *tuk-tuk* that night. He had even paid the driver my 100 *baht* fare. Your typical American, so frugal when overseas these days, is capable of genuine small kindnesses, if given half a chance.

A letter from my bank in the States arrived informing me that my last thousand dollars had been wired to my account in Bangkok. I stopped by a language institute that had offered me a job teaching English some months before. The director, a bloated Thai with sour pools of pinkish rheum collecting in the corners of his eyes, grumbled that I had caught him at a bad time, and maybe he would be able to use me sometime in the future and maybe not. He couldn't be sure. There were hordes of young Brits and Aussies and Yanks trekking off to the hinterlands with their Patpong and Soi Cowboy and Nana's Plaza girlfriends to smoke dope and copulate and goof on the wavy pristine drapery of nature, and then returning to the city broke and eager to replenish their drained wallets and empty stash pouches. They worked cheap. I envied them their release and the impudent nose they thumbed at the workaday world. They babbled of jungle visions and fondled exotic *phra phim* amulets and griped about visa hassles and the capriciousness of Thai law enforcement and bureaucratic red tape, but on the whole were no more ridiculous than your suburban American clown grilling burgers in his backyard and staring with suppressed menace at his wife's fat-ass bermuda shorts and varicose veins.

And I thought about Jack's girl at Pussy Hard Rock. There was no denying I had had some sort of "attack." Or what brought it on. One could speculate, of course, and posit what kinds of occult psychic machinery might lie behind the simple cause-and-effect. But as the days and nights after that evening wore on, the truth became simple and incontrovertible: I was heartsick. A man of fifty-four in love with a hill country whore clearly not yet twenty years of age. Whom he had never spoken even one word to. Had not been in the same room with—save for ten minutes of mental and emotional and physical disaster. I needed to see her, and I feared that if I did I might relapse, or worse. It no longer mattered much if she was a *mai kee* or not. Perhaps there was no such thing as a *mai kee*, after all. Old Fishbourne was a man in deep despair over a dead wife when he examined the woman from That Phanom.

He believed that the pig innards the charlatan on Luzon pretended to tug out of a fold in his wife's abdomen were her own cancerous bowels. And I had never had a chance to give Pong the kind of thorough gynecological examination necessary before the Delhi arms merchant whisked her away. She was shy that way and ran screaming and jumping about my lodgings when I produced the speculum. Every man, as I said, has this triangular hole in his brain that longs to be filled, completed. But no man's hole is exactly the same as another's. We're all different, absurdly so. My story here would probably strike the average Joe bellying up to the bar in Kokomo as the demented raving of a lunatic. So be it.

I wrote a note and signed it and left it on the table of my lodging house room. I did not honestly know if I would return home alive that evening. I wanted Julie to have my Ibo fertility puppets and my Korean shaman wind skates. There's not much an anthropologist can leave the daughter of a divorce, in the end. I doubted the university would want my papers. And there was nothing left in my bank account. That last grand was the silted residue of a prematurely drained IRA. Then I turned off the lights and sat in the dark and let my eyes adjust to the pair of cheap sunglasses I had picked up from a street vendor. It struck me as extraordinarily comical that I was like a man preparing to view a solar eclipse, calculating the potential retinal damage and pressing ahead just the same. Quite mad and quite in possession of himself, just the same.

*

In the murky darkness of Pussy Hard Rock I maneuvered my half-blind way to the same snuggle couch on which I'd collapsed two weeks before. It was still early in the evening and the only other customers were a couple of young German tourists wearing t-shirts that proclaimed in slick obscene mottoes that they were survivors of the greatest fuckfest since the Romans carried off the Sabine women. Jack's girl stood naked on the raised stage behind the bar, bending one knee and then the other to the beat of "Light My Fire," holding on to a pole fixed to the floor and ceiling. I fought off the impulse to tear off my dark glasses and take her in wholly. Already my heart was racing and my palms wet. The heavenly blip of white light between her thighs was muted to a gauzy glow. A plump waitress sauntered over and plopped down beside me on the snuggle couch.

"How come you got a sunglasses on?"

"The better not to see with."

"Tik no understand."

"Your name's Tik?"

"My name Tik. What your name?"

"That girl up there. What's her name?"

"What girl? Got seven girl up there."

"The one," I said breathlessly, "holding on to the pole."

"That Moi. Moi no talk girl. No hear."

"She's deaf?"

"Okay."

Only now did I notice that as she danced, the girl called Moi kept an eye on the legs of the other girls on stage, divining the rhythm of the music from their movements.

"You want Singha?"

"Sure. Bring me a beer."

"You want Moi come sit with you?"

"Please," I said, as the room commenced to tilt and spin and I summoned from the giddy depths of my being the balance and equipoise of my spirit's sea-legs and my soul's gyroscope. "Yes, please. But please ask her to put something on."

*

Moi lay on my bed that evening and many an evening after that, her legs spread in the manner of a Pussy-Blow-

Dart-Pop-Balloon sharpshooter casting a trajectory. I sat beside her on a chair behind my sunglasses. With a hand-book on International Signing picked up at a used-book stall we learned to communicate well enough that way, silently. Eventually a pink tip did emerge between her dainty nymphae and, improvising on a technique known to ancient Chinese sages as Burbling at the Jade Fountain, I managed to teach her a few basic phrases in English like "Oh thank you, but you flatter me" for the inevitable comments she was sure to receive regarding her stunning beauty and "Go fuck yourself" for anyone making a snitty comment to her about our age difference.

But learning a language is not like turning a trick, and teaching one is not easy either. Even now every syllable we attempt costs her a laborious effort, but she makes it just the same, for me. Perhaps she has a hole in her brain too, and something about me–though I cannot imagine what this could be–fits it just right. But women aren't the same as men, that much we all know. She'll never be fluent, and we've had to accept that. We were the talk of the town for a while, so to speak, once back in the States. Perhaps you caught us on the tube that afternoon Oprah set her microphone on Moi's modestly skirted lap and all of America heard her muffled pussy ask "Why is everybody in the audience so fat?" She did me particularly proud that day, for I had not taught her that expression. We had not practiced it. She had learned it on her own. I had to slap my thigh and laugh when a hefty New Jersey matron with blue hair stood up and pointed at us and howled "Ventriloquism! I saw it! He moved his lips!" Jack got wind that Moi was in America and phoned one afternoon from his home in Santa Monica. I don't know why. Perhaps he really hadn't understood she was deaf. But I was happy to have the opportunity to thank him for helping me out of Pussy Hard Rock that evening. "I couldn't have done it alone, Jack." I handed Moi the receiver and she slipped off her panties and squatted down on the mouthpiece and gazed up a me imploringly and squeaked, "It was sweet of you to call, Jack. You were a dear. I'm happily married now."

And demonstrating that old Fishbourne had not been so completely off his rocker after all helped reinstate me at Harvard. My "Talking Pussy of That Phanom" piece—much elaborated—is now often cited as a singular example of dogged pursuit of truth. But I don't much care for teaching anymore. The students these days have no imagination, no vision of the Quest. Fieldwork for them is little more than a textbook exercise. They would rather paddle a canoe up the Orinoco to undertake protein efficiency studies of Yanomamo hunting methods than follow in the footsteps of an iconoclast like my mentor. Ptah! I would rather scrub toilets in a bus station men's room. And my colleagues are no better. At cocktail parties the younger ones corner Moi in kitchen nooks and on bended knees address the most indecent proposals directly to her pelvis. She's a good sport, of course, and lets them off with a sharp knuckle-rap to the pate and a snappy *Maeng-ka-phroon! Ra-wang!* from those very same nether regions whilst hers truly stands off, nodding and winking—and Moi winking back in that way she has.

But I guess I can't blame them. Just the thought of making love to her is unutterably overwhelming. And actually doing it–my god! Once a week is almost more than my constitution can handle. And I have had to hang on to those shades. I still cannot bear to take in her full frontal nakedness. That dancing splash of unearthly white light between her thighs. We couple in the dark, like shy honeymoon lovers. Her deafness is incurable. And she will never learn to talk the way normal people do. So much for the magicians at Harvard Med. At night we lie side by side in a dark world of silence, punctuated only occasionally by tender whispers delivered up from that sweet fissure between her legs: *Please nudge me if it starts to drizzle. I so love to watch the raindrops dance on the window.* We live in a world of silence. But speech, regardless of where it proceeds from, is nothing more than manipulated sound, and sound nothing more than agitated air.

Wink.

THE GHOST STORY
COMPRESSION: A VERY SHORT STORY

I ran into H. at the Closerie. It was early in the afternoon. A gray winter day. He had his notebook and three sharpened pencils in front of him on the table. But he was staring off into space. He was not writing. He looked stumped. He had gotten a few words down. Maybe a whole line. But no more than that. He looked stumped. He had that hat on that he sometimes wore when he wrote. But it looked a little bit too big for him today. It kept slipping down over his eyes and he had to push it back up again in order to stare off into space properly.

H. was a big man but he did not look quite so big today. Maybe he was having problems at home, I wondered. He was famous for having problems at home. No, he wasn't having problems at home. Wife's fine. So is the baby. It's this shirt. And these damn trousers. Too loose.

Good for the circulation, I said. Blood flow. Free flow of thoughts. Ideas. Impressions.

No, he said. Opposite. I got this iceberg inside me. Iceberg in my heart.

Maybe you should see a doctor, I said.

A doctor, he said. He looked down at the line in his notebook. If it was a whole line. No, he said. No. Tried that. It's this iceberg. This iceberg in my heart. Everything feels so compressed.

Go fishing then. Get out of Paris. Get out of town.

No, he said. No. Tried that too. It's this damn compression. It just comes over me. I'm fine one minute and sitting here writing and one word leads to another word and then *boom*—I get so damn compressed. It comes out of nowhere. Done. Finished. Look at me. Look at this hat. It's two sizes too big. And this shirt. And these trousers. Don't even look at my shoes. Don't look under the table. I used to have the biggest feet in Paris. If I get up and take two steps I'll walk right out of them. He moaned. He groaned. It all started, he said, with that six word story business. I bet everybody I could best them. Write a whole story in only six words. Better story than anything they could come up with in only six words. And won. Hands down.

Sure, I said. I remember. I was here. *A clean, well-shaven place it wasn't.* I remember that.

No, he said. That wasn't it.

I tried again. But I couldn't remember well. We had all been drinking that afternoon. *Mendicant hits lottery. Farewell to alms.*

No, he said. That wasn't it either. Something about shoes. Baby shoes. Look at my feet. I could probably fit in them now. I get so compressed.

That's where it all started, I said. With those little six worders?

And then it spread, he said. To the stories. About that summer up in Michigan. Compression everywhere. Can't escape it. I get so compressed.

It happens to everyone, I said. Sooner or later. Look at me. Ever seen anyone so compressed?

H. stared. Squinted and stared. Like he didn't even recognize me. Like he was trying to make out something that wasn't really there.

No, he said. Not like this. It's in my stories now. Look. Here. This one about Nick and his old man. The doctor. The pregnant squaw. Uncle George. The Indian father in the bunk overhead. It's gone. I can't see it anymore.

Indian Camp, I said.

That's it. Indian Camp.

He slid his notebook across the table. I looked down at the line. The handwritten words: *Boy goes. Blood flows. Father crows.*

That's compressed, I said. That's compression.

Full blown, he said. The worst kind. Can't shake it.

You need to decompress. You've erased your best ever story so far. Compressed it till it's nothing but six words.

Cut. I cut and cut. Can't help myself. And this damn iceberg in my heart. Compression. Twenty-nine pages down to seven pages down to less than a single line.

You've got to cut out all this cutting out, I said. De-compress.

Decompress, H. said. I can't. It's gone. I just can't see it anymore. He was staring off into space again. Almost like he had never really seen me at all.

Waiter, I said, and I raised two fingers. Absinthe. Deux. One for the gentleman in the too big hat and too loose shoes. And one for the empty chair he's talking to.

ACKNOWLEDGMENTS

"Stakeouts & Stings: Four Backflung Geezer Glances"
Main Street Rag (2022)

"Pay Back"
Foreign Literary Review (2021)

"Give Piss a Chance"
Erotic Review Magazine (2021)

"Compression: A Very Short Story"
The Ghost Story (2018)
(Reprinted in *21st Century Ghost Stories* Anthology)

"The Poet, the Rapist and the Cops"
Entelechy: Mind and Culture (2006)

"Steam Irons of Desire"
Pearl (2006)

"Mai Kee"
Exquisite Corpse: Cyber Corpse (2001)

"A History of My Auto Eroticism"
Pearl (1998)
(Reprinted in *Coming Off the Line:
The Car in American Culture* Anthology)

"Penpals"
Synaesthetic (1997)

"Kimbop's Story"
Lightning & Ash (1996)

"Rose in the Steel Dust"
Timber Creek Review (1995)
(Reprinted in *The Raw Art Review* Winter 2023)

"Cave" (Originally "Deep Kimchi")
and "At Play in the Year of the Dog"
Exquisite Corpse (1995)
(Reprinted in *Thus Spake the Corpse:*
An Exquisite Corpse Reader, 1988-1998, Volume Two Anthology)

"The Assassin and the Gypsy"
Slipstream (1994)

"My First Foreign Lover and the Sea"
Furious Fictions (1993)
(Reprinted in *Uncle John's Bathroom Reader* Anthology)

"Red"
Perchan's Chorea: Eros and Exile (Watermark Press) (1991)

"Pumping Ethyl"
The North American Review (1975)